A SWORD NAMED VENGEANCE

RYAN KIRK

WATERSTONE
MEDIA

For Greg

1

No matter how many miles he traveled, Tomas couldn't outrun the ghosts of his past. They waited for quiet moments when his mind was still, lurking with the patience of the dead, for whom time had no meaning.

Tomas could never predict what summoned them. Three days ago, a loaf of fresh bread had brought his old unit back, flesh rotting from their faces as they joined him at his fire. A week back, the sound of two horses approaching had returned him to a jail cell after the war, listening to the executions through steel bars. Tonight, she sat next to him in the grass, and he swore he caught her scent on the late summer breeze.

Figments of his imagination, all. Elzeth couldn't see them. But they looked no less real for knowing it.

He worried. He didn't exhibit any signs of tics, not that anyone could see. Maybe, though, madness took more forms than he knew, and this was his.

Answers, hopefully, weren't far away. Two, maybe three days of travel.

Assuming the unexpected guest hiding in the tall grass didn't derail his plans.

Thick clouds obscured Tolkin and the stars. A dark night, perfect for mischief. Tomas had built no fire when he stopped for the day. Even a small flame could be seen for miles, and he desired no company.

Twenty paces to the south, the grass moved against the wind.

Her ghost vanished, content to wait in the shadowy corners of his mind until another quiet moment allowed her to return.

The disturbance in the grass came closer, and Tomas now heard someone crawling through the grass. They were careful, but not nearly silent enough to sneak up on a host. He lay down and closed his eyes.

It took the intruder several minutes to approach. They were too loud to be trained, so Tomas assumed they possessed an overabundance of caution. When they emerged in Tomas' camp, they went for his pack. That decision saved their life.

"It's generally considered polite to ask first," Tomas said. He opened his eyes and sat up.

The boy, or perhaps young man, jumped and scrambled a few paces back. He drew a short knife and held it between them, point toward Tomas. He didn't run, though.

"Hungry?" Tomas asked.

The young man didn't answer, his eyes darting back and forth. Then he nodded.

"Help yourself," Tomas said. "I've got plenty, and food is easy enough to come by in these parts."

The young man scrambled forward, the knife always pointed at Tomas. He grabbed the pack, then scurried a few paces away. He rummaged through the pack with one hand while threatening Tomas with the knife.

Wasn't a very trusting young man.

Perhaps with reason, though. Now that Tomas could see him better, the young man looked to be on the brink of death. A memory surfaced. Not a ghost, but a time Tomas would still rather forget. Escorting prisoners to a new camp. Bodies emaciated, sunken eyes staring into a place Tomas couldn't see.

Tomas and the others hadn't been cruel. At least, not by design. Food was scarce, and most of it went to the army. Little enough was left for the citizens the army was supposed to fight for, and even less for the prisoners it was honor-bound to care for.

That was the assignment that taught Tomas that war has no victors, no matter what historians would someday say.

The young man looked like any of those prisoners. His arms were thin enough Tomas was sure he could grab the man around the bicep and still touch thumb to finger. His eyes were like dark caves, and his hair was ragged. Around the man's right wrist was a blood-soaked bandage. Tomas' eyes narrowed. "What happened to you?"

The man made no reply as he gnawed on Tomas' food. Several of his teeth were missing.

Tomas ran his eyes up and down the man again. There were no other visible scars or bruises, but who knew what his tunic covered? "I would help, if I can."

The offer seemed to surprise the man. His head jerked up, and he seemed to see Tomas for the first time. He looked at his knife, then at Tomas. He smiled sheepishly and put the blade down.

His smile stripped years off his face. He was no more

than a boy on the cusp of manhood. Something in that grin cracked Tomas' heart.

"I suppose a knife isn't much good against you, is it?" His voice was higher-pitched, confirming Tomas' suspicion about his age.

Tomas shook his head.

"You're a solider, aren't you? One of the good ones."

The memory of the prisoners came again. "Was a soldier. Can't speak to the rest."

The boy nodded vigorously, as though Tomas had just confirmed everything he'd guessed.

"Tomas." He bowed his head, and the boy did the same.

"Pleasure," the boy replied. When he saw Tomas' reaction, he said, "I'll eat my fill, and if you'll be so kind, take some more with me. But I won't stay. Even this help will put you in danger, and I don't need any more sins on my ledger. I'd tell you my name, but that's a risk, too. I hope you'll forgive my poor manners."

"I can probably help."

The boy shook his head. "I appreciate the offer. More than you know. But I can't accept."

"You're certain?"

"It's better this way. For you, me, and the others."

Tomas leaned back on his elbows. He had a hard time believing it would be better for them to part ways. But he didn't know the situation, and more than anything, he respected the boy's right to choose his own path. Even if he disagreed. He wasn't following anyone places where they didn't want him. Not again. "As you wish. But please, help yourself to anything. You can even take the pack if you want. There's some money in the bottom."

"Truly?"

"I don't need much. A canteen and my sword should be

good to last me until the next town, and I can resupply there."

"Even if I take your coin?"

"That's easy enough to come by."

"Thank you, sir. I don't know what else to say."

"Your thanks is more than enough. Have you any news of Razin?"

His guest finished a biscuit and started another. "Nothing worth your time, I'm afraid. I've been somewhat out of touch."

Whatever the boy had been through, it had put the fear of all three hells in him. He was running away from the town Tomas hoped to find his answers in.

"Heading into trouble again, I see," Elzeth commented.

"Looks that way."

Soon enough, the boy finished his meal. "You're sure you don't mind me taking your pack? There's nothing else in here you want?"

"Nothing at all. Hopefully it lasts you for many years."

"Thanks again, sir." The boy looked around. "I suppose I best be off. If anyone asks after me, feel free to tell them I stole from you. If they find out you helped, it might mean more trouble for you."

The instructions only made Tomas more curious, but he kept his peace.

The boy stood up, and for a moment, Tolkin burst through the clouds, casting the wide prairie in its pale red light. Tomas caught his first good look at the boy and revised his estimated age down again. He couldn't be more than twelve or thirteen.

His guest smiled.

And then his head exploded, brain and bone shooting in all directions.

2

Τ he report of the rifle echoed over the rolling prairie a moment later. By the time it reached Tomas' ears, he was already moving.

Another bullet whined through the place he'd just sat.

A good shot.

Elzeth flared to life. The world became more vivid. Colors were deeper, edges sharper. Exhaustion fell from his body and mind.

The shot had come from somewhere west, which made enough sense. The boy had been fleeing the town. Poor kid hadn't been as far in front of his pursuit as he thought.

Tomas glanced up. The clouds were thick, blocking almost all of Tolkin's light. The brief illumination had been a chance event. Regardless, the shooter had acted swiftly. Given the slight but noticeable delay between the impact of the bullet and the sound of the shot, it had been at distance, too.

The darkness protected Tomas, but it hid the shooter as well.

Tomas kept to a low crouch, using the tall grass as cover as he dashed west. Every hundred paces or so, he stopped to listen. The rifle could kill Tomas several times before he got close enough to use his sword. But the shooter couldn't hit what they couldn't see.

When he thought he was close, Tomas paused for a longer time. He hadn't heard anything yet. Either the assassin was very quiet or was overconfident enough they hadn't moved.

There.

Maybe forty paces away, the killer softly cleared their throat.

Tomas lowered himself and slithered toward the sound, circling in such a way that he approached the sniper from the west.

Elzeth's assistance kept his mind sharp and his limbs strong. He parted the grass gently as he advanced, every movement premeditated. When he was close, he rose to his feet, hand on the hilt of his sword.

The assassin faced east, rifle held loosely in his hands. He knelt on one knee while he swept the barrel in a slow arc. From behind the sniper, Tomas could see what he saw, and it wasn't much. The darkness was too deep.

Though Tomas was sure that he hadn't made a sound, some animal instinct warned the shooter he was in danger. Tomas saw him tense and turn.

Too little, too late. All the rifles in the world couldn't stop Tomas when he was this close. His sword jumped from its sheath, eager for justice. With one cut the man's right arm lost all strength. The rifle dropped to the grass.

The assassin leaped at Tomas, but Tomas wasn't sure what the man intended with only an empty left hand. He snapped the flat of his blade across the man's head, knocking him straight to the ground.

The sniper had little interest in remaining down. Despite the blow, he was fighting back to his feet. Tomas stabbed down, thrusting his sword through the back of the man's left hand as he pushed himself up. The tip traveled through the man's palm and deep into the soil, pinning him in place.

The assassin's only response was a grunt of pain.

Tomas squatted down next to him. "Why did you kill the boy?"

The man made to spit in his face, so Tomas backhanded him. With Elzeth burning, the blow struck him hard enough to snap his face around.

"Who ordered you to kill him?" Tomas tried again.

This time, the man settled for damning Tomas to every imaginable hell.

As if Tomas didn't already know what awaited him on the other side of the gate.

Tomas drew a knife and spun it casually in his hand. He wanted the sniper to know he was comfortable using it. The shooter watched him but said nothing. Tomas saw the fear in his eyes, but it was controlled. "Not going to tell me anything?" he asked. "It's the difference between a quick and easy death and slow, painful one."

The man pressed his lips tightly together.

In a blink, Tomas stabbed the knife into the man's thigh. The killer groaned and his face turned pale.

But he didn't speak.

Tomas met the man's angry glare with one of his own. He twisted the knife, and the assassin snarled.

This man had killed a boy. With such a short window to

act, he'd done so without hesitation. He deserved whatever was coming to him and more.

Tomas pulled the knife out. He spun it in his hand again, flinging blood. "Once more. Why'd you kill the boy?"

The only sound to reach Tomas' ears was the breeze rustling the grasses.

Tomas had never understood such loyalty. Perhaps he was too selfish, but it seemed such a waste. Information was rarely worth a life.

He could continue. As far as these things went, he'd just barely started. But he had no stomach for it. The assassin would withstand more than Tomas was willing to do.

Tomas gave him another moment, then slid the knife between the protective ribs and into the man's heart.

Perhaps too easy of a death, but it wasn't for him to decide.

He pulled the knife out and cleaned it on the dead man's clothes. Then he removed his sword from the man's hand.

The rifle was the same model Tomas had seen all too often lately. Slowly, they were making their way into the hands of more and more people. Still far too expensive for most, but the price was coming down.

Progress, he supposed.

A quick examination of the man revealed little of interest. Tomas flipped him over and used the knife to cut through the man's tunic. He tore the fabric apart, and his stomach sank at the sight.

It probably shouldn't have been a surprise. The man had possessed some skill, and such men almost always chose a side. It also explained why the man hadn't talked. They never talked.

"I see it's another impressive mess you've gotten us into,"

Elzeth said. "And I thought visiting an inquisitor would be trouble enough."

Tomas stood up. "Would have been too easy, I suppose."

He looked down at the man again. A tattoo covered almost his entire back, marking him as one of the Family.

From the amount of ink decorating him, he had been someone important, too.

3

Tomas returned to the boy's body. Though slim, there was a chance he might reveal some crucial detail in death he held onto in life. A quick glance revealed nothing he hadn't noticed earlier. Tomas checked the boy's pockets but found them empty. Then he lifted the boy's tunic.

His torso was a mess of scars. Some were long and shallow, perhaps the work of a flail. Others were deep and made by a knife.

Tomas tugged the tunic back down and stood up. He said the old words over the boy, then looked west.

There'd never been any doubt the boy had endured a hard life. The depth of it, though, made Tomas wish he'd left the assassin alive for a bit longer. He could have shared some fraction of what the boy had lived through.

Done was done, though.

Tomas left, heading west. He walked about a mile, then found a new place to rest for the night. He didn't leave the area because of superstition, but because the corpses would attract scavengers, and he had no wish to be nearby. Once he found a good site for the evening, he lay down and closed his eyes.

Sleep took him easily, but he woke well before the rise of the sun. Not that long ago, such a short night's sleep would have bothered him. This morning he felt well rested and ready for the day.

He continued west, but angled slightly south so that he might join the main road that led into town. He walked slowly, timing his arrival so that he might reach Razin sometime after midday. By noon he found the road, and afternoon was giving way to evening when the town first came into view.

Razin didn't impress him, but then again, no town did.

It was a good-sized town, large enough that several hundred people called it home. Rumors claimed that the railroads planned on building toward Razin next summer. In response, people flocked to the town, eager to take advantage of the wealth the railroad brought wherever it laid track.

Seemed like a waste of perfectly good space to Tomas, but no one had asked him.

"Sounds quiet enough," Elzeth observed.

"Probably large enough they have their own marshal. One who gets paid enough they don't run out at the first sign of trouble."

"Not sure they're going to like having us visit."

"It could be a peaceful visit," Tomas protested.

Elzeth snorted with laughter.

Tomas watched the town for another minute, memorizing what he could. The town was laid out in a convenient grid, with one main street running north and south and another perpendicular, running east and west. It looked like most of the shops were along those two streets, although

Tomas thought he saw a few buildings too large to be houses off the main streets.

One such building was the church mission, located near the northwest corner of town. Its distinctive spire towered over the town below. It was the same design Tomas had seen in half a dozen towns on the journey out here.

He would have been surprised not to see a church mission here, but the sight still made him uneasy. Those white walls all too often concealed dark deeds.

Perhaps twenty people wandered the streets, their business carrying them from shop to shop. Tomas saw no overt signs of trouble.

Indeed, it really did look like a peaceful town.

If he was lucky, it would still be peaceful when he left. All he wanted was answers, both about the boy and his own problems.

"Not going to learn anything standing here," Elzeth said.

Tomas took one last look, then kept walking.

As he neared the outskirts of town, he saw he'd already attracted attention. A woman with a rifle walked with purpose down the street, her gaze on him. The badge on her chest reflected the sun's light as it fell.

Tomas came to a stop five paces from her.

She was short. Her head only came to Tomas' chest, and he wasn't particularly tall. Her brown hair was pulled back tightly, and he guessed they were of a similar age. A veteran, like him, but on opposite sides. No other way she could wear that badge. Already, he didn't like her.

Despite her short size, her presence filled the street. The rifle was slung over her shoulder, but Tomas had the feeling it could be up and pointed at him within a heartbeat. He gave her a deep bow, acknowledging the fact.

She returned the gesture, but not as deep.

"Greetings, marshal," he said.

"Welcome to Razin," she replied. "Name's Angela."

"Tomas."

"What brings you to Razin, Tomas?"

He considered a few answers. "A personal matter."

She didn't like that answer. She took in his appearance, noting the sword on his hip. He suspected she was making the same judgments about him he'd made about her. Their pasts were on display, if one knew how to look. Angela clearly did. "We get a fair number of your kind out here. Some are honest, looking for a new start. Others just want to cause trouble. Which are you?"

"Neither, I think."

She raised an eyebrow.

"Not looking for any trouble, but not much of a believer in new starts, either. Can't erase the past, no matter how hard some people try."

She nodded at that. Relaxed, just a bit. "There's an inn down the street on your right. Can't miss it. If you don't have coin, or are otherwise so inclined, the mission offers free beds."

"I'll check the inn," Tomas said.

The hint of a smile on her face spoke volumes about her attitude toward the mission.

Their meeting over, she made to leave. Tomas stopped her. "I came across the body of a boy yesterday, out in the prairie. He was all alone and had no supplies."

Angela grimaced. "Probably looking for Ben's place."

"Ben's place?"

"An older man. Little strange. But he offers free shelter and education to children who find their way here." When she saw the confusion on Tomas' face, she explained further. "Frontier's a dangerous place, as I'm sure you know.

Doesn't stop families from trying their luck. In this area, if the parents die, the kids end up at Ben's. He feeds 'em and teaches 'em, and whenever they want, they leave. It's a kind thing he does, and word has spread. Kids come in from all over, but sometimes, they don't make it here. Not the first time."

She gave Tomas one last look. "No trouble, okay? Razin's a nice place and I mean to keep it that way. I don't have much tolerance for any misbehavior, and it's best not to test my patience. Are we understood?"

"Yes, ma'am."

Satisfied she'd done her job, Angela turned away and walked down the street. To all the others she met, she exchanged smiles and bows.

Not many marshals cared enough to meet with visitors as they came into town. Most were just veterans looking for easy money and a bit of power as reward for their service. If trouble came calling, they went running, tails tucked between their legs.

Tomas didn't wonder if trouble had settled in Angela's town despite her efforts. She didn't seem like she knew anything about the boy, and her assumption was that he'd been running toward Razin.

But he'd been running away.

Something was rotten in this town, and Tomas meant to find it.

4

After his encounter with Angela, Tomas decided to lie low for a few hours.

He wanted to explore Razin further, to get a feel for its streets and its alleys, to understand the ebbs and flows of the place. But after Angela's interrogation, he found that he had little desire to endure the sideways glances and the well-intentioned questions of passersby curious about the new stranger in town.

Anonymity was a shield he wasn't quite ready to relinquish.

They'd all know him soon enough. Of that, there was little doubt. The town was still too small not to be cognizant of strangers. But it didn't have to be today.

The deep rumble in his stomach reminded Tomas that knowledge was not all he sought in Razin. He hadn't eaten since before meeting the boy in the fields. He walked down the street toward the inn Angela had suggested.

He bit back a groan when he entered. Although the inn was clean and had plenty of tables, the decor immediately put Tomas on edge. Old, battered swords hung from every wall, and any space not adorned with dull, chipped steel was covered in what appeared to be campaign maps. Tomas stepped toward the nearest one, and sure enough, it was covered with the familiar symbols of troop placement and movement. He was pretty sure he even recognized the battle.

He'd been there.

The whole place glorified the war. Some veterans might find a measure of peace among the mementos, but he wasn't one of them.

Tomas wondered how many inns Razin had, and wondered if Angela had recommended this over any others. He was just about to turn around and seek out the answers to those questions when a portly man came through the door behind the bar and greeted him warmly. "Well met, stranger, well met!"

He bowed far too deeply, to the point where it was no longer respect, but a caricature of it. "Welcome to my humble inn. Could it be that you have heard tales of my fine establishment while enduring long hours upon the road?" The man's eyes settled on Tomas' sword.

His grin stretched even wider, a feat that, a minute ago, Tomas would've sworn was impossible. "Or perhaps you have heard that it is within these walls that you will find a second home, a place of comfort, and a ready ear to hear all your tales?"

Tomas flashed a brief smile, only because he wasn't sure how to respond. Unfortunately, the man took it as some sort of confirmation of his wild guesses.

"My name is Callum, and it's a pleasure to meet you. Please, please, join me at the bar and I shall slake your thirst."

With words and gestures, Callum pulled Tomas in as surely as if Tomas had gotten caught in a powerful river current. Before Tomas even knew what had happened, he was seated at the bar with a mug of ale in hand.

When caught in such a current, there was little to do but let it take him where it pleased. He took a sip and let the drink relax him. He eyed the innkeeper. Callum most certainly hadn't been a soldier. There wasn't a scar to be found anywhere on his body, nor was there a single callus on his palm. The only blade Callum had ever wielded was a kitchen knife.

Still, Tomas was here, and it was as good a place as any to sleep. Place looked like it had clean beds, at least. He introduced himself and took a long sip of ale.

Callum practically bubbled with joy. "It's a pleasure, yes, it is. A true pleasure to meet you, Tomas. So, tell me, what brings you to our fair corner of the frontier?"

Tomas drank more as he considered his answer. Admittedly, after a few weeks of travel on the road, the tall stool and tasty ale were true pleasures. He shrugged. "Been wandering the last few years, traveling from town to town."

"Looking for work, or a place to settle?"

"Maybe? What kind of work is available in these parts?"

Callum looked as though he'd been waiting for Tomas to ask just that question. "Oh, you'll find a lot of the same work here that you'll find anywhere else. If you can build, there's always need for those who can help with new construction. Razin is growing, and no one can build fast enough. Otherwise, if you're just looking for some honest labor, there are several farms and ranches surrounding the town that are often eager for help."

Then Callum leaned forward and whispered, as if afraid of being overheard in an otherwise empty room. "Of course, I get the feeling that you're a man who knows his way around that sword, and if so, there's far more lucrative work to be had."

Tomas suppressed his laughter as he also leaned forward. He spoke low. "What kind of work are we talking about?"

Callum's eyes glittered. "One of the reasons this town is growing so fast is because many of the trading caravans are using Razin as a hub. There is a need for warriors to guard them on their journeys. It's usually easy work and pays well."

An interesting tidbit of information, but hardly what Tomas had hoped to learn. Still, he figured he might as well play the scene out. "And you know how to get in touch with these people?"

Of course, Callum did.

Tomas understood this inn better now. Callum was a recruiter, catching the wandering warriors to serve as guards for the traders. Tomas had no problem with the arrangement. If anything, it raised his esteem for Callum a little higher. Too many of his brothers and sisters struggled to find work after the war. Given Callum's behavior, Tomas had little doubt some of the caravans were less legal than others, but what did he care? Work was work, and out here, the law wasn't much more than a nice idea.

Callum and Tomas were just finishing their conversation when the front door of the inn opened. Two men stepped in, loud and perhaps already a little drunk. They were soldiers, or at least, they had been once. They possessed all the signs Callum lacked.

"Callum!" the men yelled in unison. The innkeeper smiled, waved, and provided introductions all around. Tomas was surrounded. The two men seemed overjoyed to meet another veteran, and the questions came quickly.

Tomas answered them as politely as he could, but extricated himself by the time the third pitcher of ale found its way before him.

He wanted a clear head, and he had no desire for these men's company. It wasn't that he disliked them. They seemed kind enough, if perhaps a little rough on the edges. But he didn't like reminiscing about times long past. He thought about them too often already.

When he got to the room Callum had given him, Elzeth asked, "You fine?"

"Will be," he replied. He stepped inside his room, locked the door behind him, and opened the window. He went to the bed and lay down. There was time for a quick rest. Once night fell, his hunt would begin.

5

Elzeth woke Tomas up several hours later. Tolkin rose high in the sky, and it looked as though it wouldn't be long before Shen joined it. The room was dark and quiet.

"Any visitors?" He suspected the answer was no. Elzeth would have woken him up, had anyone neared.

"None. I don't think any of them have even gone to sleep yet."

Tomas stood and went to the window. The streets were empty. From underneath the floorboards he heard the sounds of rumbling laughter. Callum and the others seemed to be enjoying themselves, and it sounded as though they had found more company.

Tomas didn't want to walk back through that field of battle, so he climbed out the window and dropped to the alley below. With Elzeth's help, he landed softly. He glanced both ways to make sure he hadn't been seen.

The alley remained quiet.

Tomas began his hunt, not quite sure what clues he was

searching for. He wanted to find his target quickly, but didn't know how well he was hidden.

His arrival would light the fuse on an elaborate game of cat and mouse. He was almost certain the man he sought was here. That information had been the most expensive purchase of his life. He didn't think the man would run if he knew Tomas was here, but it was possible.

Thus, it was best to find the man before word spread of his arrival. Probably a difficult task considering word spread quick through towns like this.

"What does a retired inquisitor even do?" Elzeth asked.

"Their skills aren't exactly suited for most jobs," Tomas answered.

Elzeth didn't miss Tomas' implication. "You think he went to work for the Family?"

"I hope not, but it's possible."

Tomas felt Elzeth's discontent. The sting of betrayal, of a slim dagger twisted in the back. When Elzeth spoke again, anger burned in every word. "For his sake, that better not be true."

Tomas could do little but nod. In this, there was no argument between them.

Ideally, they'd stumble across the man tonight, but realistically, Tomas expected to accomplish little more than just learn more about Razin. In the last town he'd spent any amount of time in, his lack of knowledge about the place had almost gotten him killed. He wouldn't make that mistake again.

He wandered, committing the layout of the streets to memory. That task, at least, was simple enough. Razin was almost a perfect grid. He memorized other details, too. Places where he might access the rooftops. Dark corners.

Alleys that were blocked by crates. He didn't want to fight here, but if a battle found him, he'd be prepared.

At this time of night, the streets were mostly empty. More than Tomas expected. Towns on the frontier were way stations for travelers of all stripes. As such, they were typically more active in the evenings than a city dweller from the east would expect. Here, though, the noise was contained to a few specific establishments. Almost like a bigger city. Keep the potential problems contained so the rest of the town could sleep easily.

He was impressed. For a moment he dared to ask himself what it would be like to settle here.

He couldn't quite convince himself.

He passed the stalls where trading caravans could set up shop. Any place that served as a center for trade would soon have a rail station, and with the station a whole host of problems. Tomas liked the feeling of the town tonight, but this was no place for him to settle.

More and more, he wondered if anyplace was.

He was so lost in his own thoughts that he allowed himself to be spotted by one of the only other people out and about. The man in question walked alone, a sword on his hip. As soon as he saw Tomas, he approached.

It didn't take long for the deputy's badge to reflect Tolkin's red light.

There was too much law in this town.

Tomas indulged his imagination for a moment and fantasized about running away and evading the clueless deputy. Unfortunately, it would serve no purpose. He had no doubt he could escape the deputy, but then he would have Angela looking for him when the sun rose the next morning. He braced himself for more questions.

They met in the center of the street, no more than three paces apart, too close for Tomas' liking.

The deputy was young. He barely seemed old enough to carry a sword. He introduced himself as Veric. "What business do you have being out at this hour?" the deputy asked.

The people in Razin were all far too curious. "My own."

It was the wrong answer. He knew it had been.

Veric's hand went to the hilt of his sword. "We don't tolerate troublemakers in this town," he growled. The young man had been spoiling for a fight, and Tomas had given him just the excuse he needed.

Tomas took a lazy step forward but kept his hands away from his own sword.

Veric's eyes widened. Probably wasn't used to people stepping toward him after being threatened. His gaze met Tomas', and Tomas let the deputy see the utter lack of fear in his own eyes. Veric took a step back before he consciously realized what was happening.

Tomas almost laughed at the poor man. He was so young, and he had a painful earnestness to his features. He was eager to fight, but it was because he thought that was how he could best protect his town. "Relax. I'm not out to do any harm. I had a hard time sleeping and wanted to walk for a bit."

Veric had to realize he was picking a fight he couldn't win. Now Tomas' excuse gave him a reason to back down. It was all the encouragement he needed. Veric brought his hand away from his sword.

Veric studied Tomas for another moment, then gave him a knowing nod. "You're the new arrival Angela told us about."

"I am." Tomas paused as Veric's statement sank in. "Us?"

"All the deputies."

"How many of you are there?"

"Four, and her."

Tomas frowned. "That's a lot of deputies."

Veric shrugged, now clearly at ease. He'd managed to forget threatening Tomas just a few minutes ago. "We're growing fast, and she always claims that she would rather have too many deputies than not enough. When the larger caravans arrive, it's nice to have everyone around."

"The town can afford you all?"

"With the coin the caravans bring in, yeah."

Tomas grunted, then looked around the quiet town. "Seems she takes her work pretty seriously."

Veric nodded, perhaps a bit too eagerly. "She's great. I can never remember Razin being as lawless as some of the stories you hear from further west, but ever since she's started, it's become a really nice place to live."

"You grew up here?"

"For the past four years. My pa brought us not long after the first houses started going up. Best decision he ever made."

"Anything else I should know about this town?" Tomas didn't think he'd actually learn anything useful, but it didn't hurt to ask.

"Nothing comes to mind. So long as you don't cross Angela, I think you'll find this a pleasant place."

"Thanks for the advice."

Before Tomas could say farewell to Veric, there was the sound of a door slamming. In the quiet of the night, it sounded like it was right next to them, but it could have been hundreds of feet away.

Both Tomas and Veric turned toward the sound.

A woman screamed, not in pain, but in terror.

They ran toward the sound, Veric a step ahead of Tomas. They turned a corner and came upon a woman in her bedclothes, eyes wide. When she saw Veric, she pointed down the street, at nothing Tomas could see. "He took my son!" she cried.

6

The woman broke down in tears. A man came stumbling out of the house, his face looking like it had been rearranged by a brick. Blood poured freely from his nose, and one eye was swollen shut.

"Where's your son?" Veric asked.

The man spit out a tooth. "Man dressed in black grabbed him. Didn't see his face. He ran north."

Veric nodded. "I'll get him. Stay here."

The deputy ran north. Tomas looked between the pursuing deputy and the broken family. The parents held each other tightly, their bodies shaking.

Who kidnapped a child in a town like this? Big as the place was for a frontier town, it wasn't big enough to hide a child. If Angela was as good as Veric thought she was, she'd have every nook and cranny in every house explored by the end of day tomorrow.

Whoever it was, they knew how to fight. The man wouldn't look normal for a week or more.

Which meant Veric might be in trouble.

Tomas hesitated. Action now meant throwing himself

into another mess, and it wasn't the reason he was here. If anything, helping Veric risked spooking the man Tomas had come here to find.

"Just go after him already," Elzeth said.

The encouragement pushed Tomas past his doubt. He chased after Veric.

The deputy was briefly pausing to glance down every street and alley, so Tomas caught up to him quickly enough. Veric shook his head. "It might be dangerous."

Tomas ignored the young man. Elzeth burned gently, sharpening his hearing. He closed his eyes and focused.

To the east. The muffled sounds of struggle. The child fought back.

Tomas opened his eyes and pointed. "They're that way."

Veric frowned. "What?"

"Go!"

Veric obeyed, and Tomas let him lead the way. Two blocks later, Veric heard the sounds as well. He sprinted faster, and in less than a minute they found the kidnapper in an alley. As the father had described, the man was covered in dark clothing, and black fabric covered all his head, leaving only a little slit for the eyes. He was struggling with a boy, older than Tomas had expected.

The boy was putting up a decent fight. His arms and legs churned, wildly flailing at whatever of the kidnapper's body parts he could reach.

When Veric and Tomas came in sight, the kidnapper changed tactics. He delivered a blow to the side of the boy's head, knocking him out. The boy folded, and the kidnapper let him fall to the ground. He turned to flee, but Veric was having none of it. The deputy drew his sword and charged in, unleashing a battle cry loud enough to be heard across Razin.

Tomas' stomach twisted.

The kidnapper's blow to the child's head had been quick and precise. Measured, despite the violence of the action. Veric, though, charged with his sword held low and on the right side. Tomas found no fault with the deputy's form. His training was evident. But his lack of experience was, too. Tomas suspected Veric had forgotten they were fighting in an alley. Sweeping cuts would be next to useless here.

The kidnapper shifted slightly to his left and drew a long dagger. Veric altered course slightly, following the kidnapper's lead.

The fool didn't even realize he'd already lost the fight.

One pass decided the matter. The kidnapper left himself open and Veric cut. His sword dug into the wall of the house on his right and stuck there. He stumbled right into the kidnapper's dagger. He grunted, and the kidnapper gently pushed him away. The deputy took several halting steps back, then collapsed to the ground, back against the wall. He stared at nothing, eyes wide. His hand was clenched to his side and his breath came hard.

Tomas advanced, sword held in front of him.

Veric's eyes followed him. "Don't," he said. "He's too good."

"Save your strength."

The kidnapper had left himself in a predicament. The boy was unconscious but flat on his back. He couldn't safely grab the boy without Tomas cutting him. But he couldn't defeat Tomas.

Fortunately, the man didn't know that.

The kidnapper advanced, his knife a blur in the dark of the alley.

Tomas didn't let his enemy bait him into a mistake. The far greater length of his sword kept him out of the kidnapper's range. Despite the obvious openings, Tomas never extended himself. He continued his advance, forcing the kidnapper back one step at a time.

Five more steps, and Tomas would be safely between the man and his victims.

The kidnapper realized it, too. He growled, the sound coming from deep in his throat. Then he dropped into a crouch, balanced on the balls of his feet.

Tomas swore.

He'd seen that fighting style before.

The man launched himself, but not at Tomas. He angled at the wall on Tomas' left. and kicked off it.

Tomas twisted, but he'd been caught by surprise. The kidnapper blocked Tomas' cut with his forearm. Tomas discovered then the man wore some sort of vambrace underneath his long-sleeved tunic.

The long dagger came for Tomas, and Elzeth flared up.

The dagger slowed and Tomas twisted away.

The kidnapper kept close, though. He'd worked his way inside Tomas' guard and had no intent of relinquishing the advantage. He stabbed at Tomas, the dagger searching for any vital organ. Tomas twisted and backed up, avoiding anything worse than a shallow cut.

Tomas let go of the sword with his left hand as the kidnapper backed him into a wall. He flailed for the dagger hand, deflecting it away from his body. Tomas got a grip on the man's wrist. They grappled for control of the dagger, and Tomas finally put an end to it by slamming his forehead into the man's nose. He heard and felt it crack.

Their positions reversed. The kidnapper stumbled back, and Tomas pursued.

Tomas wasn't sure what had changed. As much as the broken nose had to hurt, he didn't believe he'd done any meaningful damage. But the man turned tail and ran. Tomas was about to pursue when a groan from Veric stopped him cold.

Pursuit could wait.

Tomas returned to the deputy and kneeled next to him. He didn't ask to see the wound. Studying it would be a waste of time.

Instead, he ripped fabric from Veric's tunic and wrapped it around the deputy's waist. It wasn't much, but hopefully it would staunch the bleeding.

The sounds of running feet meant help was on the way. Angela and the other deputies, unless he missed his guess. He stood up and examined the scene. There would be a lot of questions. But the boy was safe, and although he couldn't say the same for Veric, at least the deputy wouldn't be attacked any more.

Elzeth slowly settled but remained ready. Tomas looked out the alley in the direction the man had fled.

"It's been a long time since we've seen that style," Elzeth said.

Tomas had just been thinking the same.

It was a unique fighting style, only taught to one group of people Tomas was aware of.

Inquisitors of the church.

7

Angela's eyes flared when she saw Tomas standing in the alley over her injured deputy. She had her sword in hand in a blink, and Tomas feared he would soon have another fight on his hands. She ran at him, fearless.

Veric saved him from the fight. The deputy found the strength to raise his hand and stop Angela's charge. "He saved me," Veric croaked.

Angela looked between the two men. Her decisions came quickly. "Veric, take it easy. Tomas, get out of the way, but don't you dare leave this alley."

Tomas gave the marshal a quick bow, then retreated the same way the kidnapper had left the alley. He gave a brief thought to pursuit, but by now the man would have disappeared. Best to remain, follow Angela's orders, and see what came of the evening. He leaned against one of the buildings and waited.

In the space of a few minutes, the alley transformed from a quiet, shadowy path to a well-lit hive of activity. Nearly a dozen people crammed into the narrow corridor, several of them holding lanterns overhead. All the deputies appeared to be present, all of them young men like Veric. Other townspeople were also part of the posse.

Angela directed them all as well as any officer Tomas had ever served under. Her calm voice could be heard over the din of half-whispered conversations. Every order served a purpose. Veric was cared for. The injured deputy was loaded on a stretcher and hauled to the local doctor, but not before he spoke briefly with the marshal.

The boy received even more attention. Before long he came to and was reunited with his worried parents. There were plenty of tears there, but Tomas noted that the boy's father's right eye was now swollen completely shut. He didn't look like much of a fighter, but he hadn't let the kidnapper escape without a fight.

"Seems odd, a kidnapper breaking into a house to kidnap a child while the parents are around," Tomas said to Elzeth.

"Humans are bizarre creatures," Elzeth countered.

Despite the dismissive answer, Tomas felt Elzeth's own curiosity.

Something rotten festered in this town, but Tomas never would have guessed it by watching the scene before him. As the boy and Veric were cared for, the crowd began to disperse. Angela sent a couple of pairs of people out to search for the kidnapper, but from the tone of her voice, she didn't expect them to find anything.

She impressed him, though. An unusual situation, and she'd thought quickly on her feet. The search was less about finding the criminal and more about giving the citizens something to do. A better officer than most he'd served under, he decided.

Shame they'd been on opposite sides.

As he watched her, one of her deputies kept an eye on him. No doubt, she didn't completely trust him. He suspected if he made the slightest move out of the alley, he'd find that rifle of hers trained on him before long.

So, he waited.

Soon, she ordered the last of her deputies out of the alley. In a few minutes, search groups would begin returning with word of their failure. But for now, they were alone.

"Is he going to make it?" Tomas asked.

"Not sure," Angela admitted. "I'm not a doctor. Wound didn't look like it hit anything vital, but I can't be sure. You the one who bandaged him up?"

Tomas nodded once.

"Thanks. If he does make it, he'll have you to credit."

Tomas shook his head. "He shouldn't have charged in. He was outclassed from the start but didn't see it."

Angela narrowed her eyes, silently challenging his judgment. "Veric's a skilled sword."

"Decent," Tomas admitted. "But not good enough."

"Tell me what happened."

Tomas did, starting his story with the conversation with Veric. As annoyed as he might have been at the time, the fact he'd been with the deputy when this all happened saved him a world of trouble now.

Angela let him tell the story, her whole body focused on him. He told it quickly. When he finished, she chewed on it in silence. He knew, without her saying a word, that he'd left too much out.

"For the most part," she began, "that matches what Veric told me." Her dark eyes settled on him, and he felt her peeling away the layers of anonymity he tried to wrap around himself. "He also told me you were one of the best swords he'd ever seen."

"He was injured, and it was dark."

Tomas' attempt at self-deprecating humor didn't even get her to crack a smile. She crossed her arms. "This is when you tell me who you are."

At either end of the alley, people were beginning to gather once again as the first search parties returned. Deputies kept the alley clear, but Angela wouldn't have long. She wasn't the only one with questions, though.

"What's going on in this town?" Tomas asked. It was a clumsy redirection, but time was his ally right now, not hers.

"What do you mean?"

"That was no random kidnapping."

He was just guessing, but he saw the flicker of surprise on her face. She knew something. "Why not?"

Tomas wished he knew whether he could trust her. Maybe if he extended a little trust, she would return it. "The man I fought tonight was an inquisitor."

This time, there was no hiding the surprise on her face. "You think the inquisition is in my town?"

"No." When Tomas had first come across the inquisitor he now sought, they'd crossed blades a half-dozen times. Tonight's opponent hadn't been the right man. Trained in the same style, yes, but different. "Not a full inquisition, but an inquisitor."

"You expect me to believe that?"

"Go to the church. Look for a man with a broken nose."

The crowds were growing larger. Almost everyone's eyes were on the two of them now. The whole town would know him on sight by tomorrow.

"How do you know you fought an inquisitor?"

"They're trained in a unique style."

"Who are you, that you would recognize that?" He saw it

in her eyes. She suspected. All the pieces were there, and she was plenty smart enough to put them together.

"Just a retired soldier. Trying to find some answers from the past. Looking for a man I used to know."

She tapped her foot as she stared at him. The alley was getting louder as the groups on either end started updating the deputies. Her time was running out. "I should lock you up. Solves quite a few problems."

"I'd prefer it if you didn't."

"Will you leave town?"

"Not until I see if I can find the man I'm searching for."

Her foot tapped harder. But, as before, she made her decision quickly.

"I'm not going to arrest you. Near as I can tell, you haven't done anything illegal, and Veric claims you saved his life. Doesn't feel right locking a man up for that. But I want to see you in the afternoon. I've got more questions for you, and I'll be looking for better answers."

He bowed again and turned to leave.

"And Tomas?"

"Yes?"

"No more trouble before we meet again. Next time we cross paths like this, I'm not going to be so lenient."

8

Tomas returned to Callum's inn and climbed into his room via the window. He looked around. Near as he could tell, no one had been within while he was gone. Shen's blueish light faded as it set for the night. Before long, the sun would be up.

As good a time as any to sleep. He had the feeling the morning would be a busy one around town, and he had no desire for extra attention. He collapsed into the bed and was asleep in moments.

Tomas woke to the sun pouring through his window. He sat up, yawned, and stretched. Given how late he'd gone to bed, he hadn't been asleep too many hours. But he felt well-rested, as he did almost every morning now. Though he always fell asleep quickly, he very rarely felt exhausted. Just one of the questions he hoped to ask when he found the man he sought.

Then the scent of his own odor hit him. He'd been weeks on the road, and he'd been so focused on his own worries, he'd paid no mind to cleaning himself up. No wonder Angela was skeptical of him.

He ran through his forms first, waking up his body and sharpening his mind. Once done, he made his way through the inn toward the bath. He'd barely made it halfway before he ran into Callum. "The baker was in here earlier this morning, looking for you. Half his face is bruised, but he didn't want to tell me why." The innkeeper eyed him suspiciously. "Also told me there wouldn't be any fresh bread from his place today. You're not causing trouble, are you?"

Elzeth chuckled as Tomas protested his innocence. It was clear Callum was skeptical of Tomas' claims. Eventually, he let Tomas continue to the bath, but only after issuing another set of stern warnings.

"I'm starting to think people in this town don't trust me much," Tomas grumbled under his breath.

"One of the first places where it seems most people have their heads on straight," Elzeth said.

Tomas' complaints faded the moment he stepped into the bath Callum's maid had prepared. At this time of day, it was empty, everyone else having completed their morning ablutions several hours ago. The water was hot, and Tomas sank in and soaked. The dirt lifted off his skin, and the warmth of the water eased the knots in his muscles. He closed his eyes and sighed.

By the time he emerged from the bath, he was a new man. Clean and shaven, he hoped he would make a better impression on the citizens of Razin. Not because he cared about their opinion, but because their constant glances and suspicious looks grew old.

Angela had requested he visit in the afternoon, and it was still too early. He had a good guess who the baker was and decided that would be his first stop. He left Callum's inn and began searching the main streets for a bakery.

The first one he stepped in wasn't the one he wanted.

There were, it turned out, two, and it was the other one that was closed. Unlike Callum, the owner of this bakery knew why, too. The man's son had almost been kidnapped. It didn't take long for the baker to realize Tomas had been the one who saved the boy, and he emerged from the bakery with a loaf of bread given in thanks.

He couldn't say he cared for the attention, but he wasn't a man to turn down food freely offered.

He didn't even make it to the other bakery. Halfway there, the baker's family stopped him. Tomas got the sense they'd been in the streets searching for him.

The whole family bowed deeply toward Tomas, a display that brought a flush to his cheeks. Other passersby noted the interaction, and Tomas caught a few other small bows in his direction.

"There's no need for any of that," he said.

The family ignored him and held their bows. Tomas stepped toward them and gently lifted the father up by the shoulder. They stood face to face, and tears were streaming from the man's eyes. He nodded quickly, unable to speak.

Tomas' heart twisted. "Truly, there's no need for any of that. I'm just glad that your boy is fine."

"If there's anything we can do for you," the baker said, "all you have to do is ask."

"Could you tell me what happened last night?"

All four of them moved to the side of the street, where they would be out of the way. The father recounted the story quickly enough. He'd woken up early, as he did every day, only to bump into the cloaked man carrying their son from the home. The baker had fought, but as his face so clearly attested, he was not a fighting man. The fight woke the mother, though, who had then screamed for help.

"Do you have any idea why someone might want to kidnap your child? Do you owe money to anyone?"

The father shook his head. "The marshal asked us the same, and we've been thinking about it all morning, but nothing comes to mind. I don't even think anyone in town dislikes my bread."

Elzeth chuckled at that. "Sorry," the sagani apologized. "But if that was the reason for the kidnapping, all hope for humanity would be lost."

There had to be a reason, though. Tomas was sure the culprit had been an inquisitor. "Have you ever had any problems with the church?"

The baker shook his head again. "We're not believers, but most people in town aren't. Why?"

Tomas ignored the question, deep in his own thoughts. He recalled the young man he'd come across in the prairie. Then he looked at the baker's boy. They were a few years apart, the baker's son younger. But maybe the kidnapping didn't have anything to do with the baker. Maybe it was all about the boy.

Tomas squatted down so he was at eye level with the boy. He gave a short bow of greeting. "Name's Tomas. I'm glad to see you're doing well."

The boy bowed in response, slightly deeper, as befitting the recognition of an elder. "Hadwyn."

He seemed nervous, but Tomas supposed that was to be expected after such a night.

"Hadwyn, have you ever met a boy who was a little taller and older than you?" Tomas described the young man he'd come across.

Hadwyn's eyes lit up. "That sounds like Robick!"

"Who's Robick?" The question came from the baker.

Hadwyn looked between all the adults. "He was one of

Ben's boys. He was real tough, but really nice. He and I were friends for a while, but then Ben said he ran away. I haven't seen him for months."

Tomas shot the parents a questioning look. The baker answered. "Ben runs a place for lost children on the edge of town. He's a bit odd, but he does well by the kids."

Tomas had no problem remembering the scars on Robick's back. He had the suspicion that Robick hadn't actually run away. And the young man had been concerned about "others." No doubt, he meant the others at Ben's place.

A refuge for children, or something else altogether?

Tomas planned on finding out.

A tug on his sleeve brought him back to the present. Hadwyn was looking at him with an expectation that broke his heart. "Have you seen Robick? I want to play with him again."

Tomas looked up at the parents, and they saw the pain in his eyes. He gave them the smallest shake of his head, and they seemed to understand. But Tomas couldn't bring himself to lie.

The baker saved him. He wrapped his strong arms around his son and held him close. "Don't worry, Hadwyn. People will keep looking for him. He's out there, somewhere."

Someday, the baker would have to break the news to his child. But not today, not when the world already seemed so dark.

The mother peeled her child away, and the baker spoke with Tomas alone. They spoke in low voices. "He's dead, isn't he?"

"I came across his body outside of town. Looked like he'd seen some pretty rough days."

"You think it had something to do with Hadwyn?"

Tomas shrugged. "Don't think it was random."

Fear flashed in the baker's eyes, but he doused it quickly. "Word is, you're pretty good with that sword. You going to do something about it?"

"Might."

The baker nodded. "Then I'll leave you with my thanks. If you ever need anything, anything at all, don't hesitate."

"I appreciate that."

They parted ways as friends, but Tomas' mind had already moved on. He had a little time before Angela would expect him. Perhaps a visit to Ben's home was in order.

9

Thanks to his previous excursion, Tomas had a good idea where Ben's place was. In the southeast corner of town there was a walled property. It wasn't that much larger than other lots, nor was the home within the walls remarkable in any way Tomas had seen. But it was the only walled lot in town.

Tomas' guess only took a few minutes to prove. He moseyed toward that corner of town, and it wasn't long before the sounds of children playing filled the air. They came from behind the wall.

When the property came into view, Tomas was surprised to see the main gates open, and children running in and out freely.

Elzeth sensed his surprise. "Not quite the secret and dangerous place you were imagining?"

"Not quite."

As he reached the main gate, he almost ran into two boys sprinting out of it. Tomas danced nimbly out of the way, and he thought he heard an apology halfheartedly shouted as the boys sprinted down the street.

Inside the walls, the place was a hive of activity. More than a half-dozen children played in the yard. One large silver maple tree stood in the corner of the property, and a small wooden platform had been built among its sturdy branches. Tomas watched a tiny girl, who couldn't have been more than five or six, pull herself up a rope that went through a hole in the floor of the platform. The rope climb was almost too much for her, but she seemed determined to avoid the ladder that provided the easier way up.

He only watched for a minute, but that was enough.

All the children here looked well fed and happy. And clean enough, although Tomas suspected that any struggle to keep these children clean was a losing battle. None of them seemed to have anything in common with Robick.

Tomas looked around the yard again. Robick would have been one of the oldest children here, if not the oldest.

He'd come here expecting to find...something, he supposed. Some evidence of wrongdoing. But this place didn't feel like that. It felt good. Like a place where seeds of hope were nurtured and cared for.

The front door of the house opened, and a woman came out. She wore a shapeless dress, now covered in flour. Her light hair was pulled up in a tight bun. She struck Tomas as unremarkable, until she smiled at him.

It was a gentle smile, the sort he associated with a person incapable of cruelty.

He offered a bow, and suddenly the sword on his hip seemed clumsy and tasteless. If the woman thought so, though, she gave no clue.

"Afternoon, ma'am. My name is Tomas, and I was looking for Ben. I've heard he runs this place."

The mention of Ben's name made her smile grow even wider. Tomas glanced at her hand but saw no ring.

"I'm afraid my husband isn't here right now," the woman said, brushing some of the flour off her dress, "and I'm sorry to say I'm not quite sure when he'll return."

Tomas thought he caught a hint of worry in her voice.

"My name is Olena, and I welcome you here." She ran her eyes quickly up and down him, and they stopped for a moment on his sword. "Is there anything I could help you with?"

Tomas faltered. He'd come here expecting some sort of confrontation. He said the first lie that came to mind. "I've just recently arrived in Razin, and I'd heard about what you and Ben do here. It made me curious, and I was of a mind to indulge my curiosity."

Olena opened her arms out wide. Her smile never left her face, and Tomas had the feeling she was the sort of woman who didn't even kill spiders in her house. She probably captured them and moved them outside. "And what do you think?"

"I've never seen anyplace like it in all my travels," Tomas replied truthfully.

She beamed at that.

Before Tomas could ask any questions, two girls ran up to Olena and wrapped themselves around her legs. Through tears, they told Olena of a boy who hadn't let them play with some toy. Tomas could barely understand them through their wails.

Olena, however, could, and before long, she had them calmed down. She looked up at Tomas. "Will you excuse me for a moment?"

She took the two girls to one corner of the yard, where a boy had collected an impressive assortment of toys. Olena mediated between the three children.

"What do you think?" he asked.

"It's peaceful here. Truly peaceful." There was no trace of Elzeth's usual biting sarcasm.

"Agreed."

Olena returned alone, the three children now playing, if not completely willingly, at least peaceably, behind her. "Sorry about that."

"No apologies necessary. If you don't mind me asking, what made you and Ben decide to do this?"

"I like to think it's because I made Ben do it. He'd tell you we decided it together, but I think that's just because he doesn't want to give me all the credit." She spoke as someone who had answered the question before. "I only met Ben a few years ago, out east, but we fell quickly in love. We were married a few months after we met and came out west."

Her face clouded, but only for a moment. "Ben didn't want children, but he was also really good with them. He has a gift for understanding people. It all started as a bit of an accident, really. We came across a child begging a few towns over. His parents had died in some feud, and no one in the town wanted to take him in. I convinced Ben we could care for him. It just kind of grew from there."

"So, what exactly do you do?"

"We give them beds and food. Ben teaches them. We try to find them apprenticeships when they come of age."

Tomas gestured to the gate. "A couple of children ran out of here just as I arrived."

Olena nodded. "They do, sometimes. That's one of Ben's rules. Everything here is by choice. Children can come and go as they please. They can attend lessons or choose not to. But no matter what, they have a safe place here until they turn sixteen. Then they need to find an apprenticeship."

"How many stay?"

"Most," Olena said. "A few have left us early, for various reasons, but not often."

"It seems a wonderful thing you do here."

"Thank you."

"Where is Ben?"

She shrugged. "I'm not sure. We heard a rumor from one of our new children a couple of days ago. Something that might have to do with some of our kids. Ben went to investigate. He told me he might be gone a few days."

Olena worried about Ben, but Tomas noted that she didn't seem overly concerned.

He decided not to press for more details. He'd seen enough to know his initial suspicions of this place were unfounded.

Had the rumors had anything to do with Robick?

Tomas wondered if Ben was dead, too. Killed by the Family sniper before he even found Robick. Or perhaps after. That would explain the boy's fear. He didn't have the heart to tell this woman her husband might be in danger, or worse.

"Well, thank you for indulging my curiosity. I'm in town for at least the next few days. Would you mind if I stopped by again?"

"So long as you're willing to help out with some chores, come by anytime," she said.

Instinctively, Tomas wanted the best for her. As he left, he hoped that his fears about Ben were unfounded, and that her husband would return to her soon.

She deserved no less.

10

The jail was across town, on the east-west main street, close to the western edge of Razin. Tomas made his way there slowly. The heat of the day had passed, and the streets held a fair number of people. Tomas let the sounds of the town wash over him. Two men were arguing to a third about the appropriate placement of a property line. A woman haggled with the butcher over the price of meat.

He sensed no danger. Most everyone carried a knife of some sort, and one or two of the men had old, battered swords hanging from their hips, but that was all. He saw no sharp-eyed sentinels. Hells, he didn't even think he saw many soldiers. One woman walked with a limp that might have been earned in battle, and a few men carried visible scars, but Tomas saw nothing that alarmed him.

A normal town.

At least as normal as existed out here.

He reached the jail and paused. There was still some chance Angela might try to arrest him for last night's trouble.

Nothing for it, though. He opened the door and stepped in.

The jail was as clean as he'd expected. Anyone who kept a frontier town this quiet kept their space clean, too. Angela reminded him of the better officers he'd served under in the war. Orderly minds, orderly spaces, and the ability to bring order to the soldiers under their command. Such officers weren't common, in Tomas' experience. They weren't necessarily who you wanted to have in command in desperate situations, either. Competence and creativity didn't necessarily go hand in hand.

But they were reliable and predictable, and sometimes, that was just what a soldier needed.

A large, sturdy oak desk dominated the front room of the jail. A deputy sat behind it and greeted Tomas. He gestured further back. "First room on the left. She's expecting you."

She'd heard him come in, because by the time he reached her door, she was already up. All Tomas got was a glance at her office before she waved for him to follow her. Her personal office was even tidier than the rest of the place. Together, they walked deeper into the building.

Four heavy doors stood open, and Tomas got his first look inside Razin's jail cells. They were plain, windowless rooms with thick walls. Clean, though. Much nicer than some cells Tomas had found himself in.

Fortunately, Angela didn't lead him into one of them.

She led him instead to another thick door at the end of the hall. She opened it, revealing an outdoor practice yard. It was an almost intimate space, not more than ten feet to a side, but the high wall around it made it seem smaller than it was.

Angela shut the door behind them and gestured to the practice weapons. "Pick one."

Tomas gave her a sideways glance. "What if I just told you I was a host? Could we skip this?"

Her smile transformed her face and forced him to shift his opinion of her. He'd thought her hard and efficient. Now he saw a hint of something more. A playfulness he wouldn't have guessed existed. "Not a chance. I've never had the opportunity to duel a host, and I'd like to see how long I last."

The answer shifted his opinion of her further. Even a duel with wooden weapons was an act of trust. They were no less lethal for being dull. If she knew he was a host, her friendly challenge was as good as saying she trusted him with her life.

Either that, or she was very good.

Or overconfident.

Tomas' curiosity was piqued. He went to the wall and found a sword he liked. Angela did the same. They squared off against one another.

She attacked.

Tomas had expected her to test his skills with a handful of easy exchanges, but she had other plans.

He wasn't sure he'd ever seen a style quite like hers. Her feet moved quickly, dancing across the dirt of the practice yard, lighter than a bird. When her practice sword cut at him, he was reminded almost of a hummingbird. The cut looked gentle, but it was precise, and *fast*.

Tomas scrambled backward. When he parried a cut, the wooden sword vibrated in his hand. There was far more power in those swings than he expected.

Worse, Elzeth remained still, holding back any extra strength or speed.

Her sword smacked against his left arm, and he swore.

She immediately halted her assault and her eyes narrowed.

Elzeth chuckled.

"Are you actually a host?" she asked, doubt in her eyes.

"You going to help this time?" Tomas asked Elzeth.

Elzeth stirred to life, laughing all the while. "Couldn't help myself."

"Try again," Tomas said to Angela.

She seemed to barely need the encouragement. She attacked again, every bit as fast as before.

Elzeth burned brighter, and Tomas had no problem tracking Angela's moves. For a moment, he admired her form, the way the subtle shifting of her weight gave her far more power and speed than anyone would expect. It was a demanding style, one that relied on a perfection of movement.

It wasn't enough against him, though. He found the gaps in her defense, and she couldn't guard them quickly enough. He caught her on the upper thigh.

They disengaged, and he was surprised to see the smile still wide on her face.

"Remarkable," she said. "You were trained before you became a host, right?"

He nodded. The guess was reasonable enough, but it was still unusual for anyone to put the pieces together so quickly.

"I couldn't tell any difference until it was too late. No wonder both the armies wanted hosts on their side." Angela returned her practice sword to the wall, and Tomas followed suit. Then she turned to face him. "We got off on the wrong foot, and I apologize. I spent the morning with Veric, and after hearing his side of the story again, I think you prevented him from making some fatal mistakes last night. I misjudged you when you came into town."

Tomas imagined what he must have looked like that day and found he couldn't blame her. Weeks on the road stripped away a lot from a person. Combined with his sword and demeanor, he'd probably suspect himself, too.

Angela continued, "I won't demand you tell me your purpose for visiting, if you would rather not, but I know you know something you aren't telling me."

He liked her. He wanted to believe she was honest and good. But he couldn't risk getting run out of town. So, he tested her. "I discovered the name of the boy I found dead outside of town. Robick."

Her surprise wasn't faked. "The boy who ran away from Ben's months ago?"

He nodded.

She thought out loud. "Hadwyn and Robick were friends." She looked away, staring at nothing, then back to him. "It wasn't a coincidence, was it?"

He believed her. She wasn't bought, as so many marshals were. "I didn't just find Robick. He was killed." He told the story, not forgetting to tell her of the sniper's Family affiliation.

Angela sat on a small bench pushed up against the wall. He could see her thinking the problem through. "But you're sure Hadwyn was kidnapped by an inquisitor?"

"I am."

"Which would imply that the church and the Family are working together. But I can't believe that. It wasn't that long ago a feud between the two sides burned down an entire town." She pressed her palms against her eyes. "You'll forgive me if I don't believe you."

She'd come to the same question he had, and neither of

them had an answer. "Wouldn't believe it myself if I hadn't seen it with my own eyes," Tomas said.

"No matter how you cut this puzzle, the pieces don't come together." Angela switched from sitting to standing, pacing back and forth. "We've got to be missing something that ties this all together."

"You've got another problem, too," Tomas said.

Angela glared.

"Ben's been gone for a few days. He told his wife he was searching for Robick. Given that we know what happened to the boy, it makes me worry something happened to him."

Angela clenched her fists. "There's not much I can do for him. Without something more, I can't spare the men to go searching. He could be anywhere."

Tomas had worried that would be her answer.

She thought for a moment, then stood up straighter. "First things first. Will you take me to the site where Robick was killed? Maybe I can identify the Family member."

"You don't think predators have gotten to him?"

She shook her head. "There's a fair number of sagani in these parts, which keeps most of the predators at bay. And no one's come into town from the east since you arrived, so no kind stranger should have buried it."

Tomas told her he would. Anything that got them closer to answers served him well.

And perhaps on the ride, he could get her to tell him the identity of the man he was looking for.

———

11

Angela loaned Tomas a horse from their stable, which was, in itself, an expression of her trust in him. Even though she armed herself with a rifle for their journey, there wasn't much to stop him from riding away.

Her trust unsettled him.

Were he in her place, he wasn't sure he would be capable of the same.

Maybe he'd been alone for too long with only the ghosts of his memories. Maybe he'd become too mistrustful of others.

They rode out of town in silence, following the same trail that Tomas had walked a couple of days earlier. Angela maintained the silence until they were well beyond the last house.

He thought he'd be the one to attempt to dig information out of her.

It seemed, though, that she had the same plan.

"You still don't trust me, do you?" she asked.

He saw no point in dancing around the answer. She

already knew the truth. "Can't say I do, no."

"Is it because I fought for the other side?"

Tomas almost shook his head, then stopped. "I'd like to say 'no,' but that might be part of it. Mostly just have trouble trusting authority at all."

"Spoken like a true child of the rebellion." From most, Tomas would have expected bitterness in such a statement, but he didn't hear any in Angela's voice. To her, it was nothing more than a fact.

Before he could answer, she changed the direction of the conversation. "So, why are you here?"

He smiled at her tenacity. "Thought you weren't going to ask that."

She mirrored his smile. "Never said I wouldn't ask. Said you didn't have to tell if you didn't want."

Should he tell her? Telling her the truth still might get him run out of town. He hadn't been in Razin long enough to know how the power was balanced.

Despite his misgivings, though, Angela was winning him over. She seemed like someone he could trust. He wanted to trust her.

"You're not like most of the other soldiers that have come through here," Angela said, interrupting his deliberation.

Tomas grunted. "Most aren't hosts."

She shook her head. "Not that. You. Almost every soldier coming through here falls into one of two camps. They're either running from something, or they're stuck trying to relive the days of glory."

"Tried running for a while," Tomas admitted. "Didn't work so well."

"I didn't think you were a runner," Angela said. "Not when I first met you. That's why I sent you to Callum's place.

He's a bit of a pain, but he does connect soldiers with meaningful work."

"Keeps them out of your town?"

Her grin was answer enough. "No glory days for you, though?"

Tomas' smile faded at that. "No glory in what I did. Nothing to relive."

She studied him then, openly and for nearly a full minute. "You were in one of the unnamed units, weren't you?"

He gave her one brief nod. "Not at first. Grew up orphaned in one of the sword schools. Tried avoiding the service, but I kept getting in trouble with the law. Fighting in the war was my only way out. Didn't become a host until about a year later. Once command discovered my ability, they moved me."

It was far more than he meant to say, but Angela gave him a small bow of her head, as if to acknowledge his experience.

That small gesture slipped her past the rest of his defenses. Most soldiers from the other side would have tried to kill him on the spot. And they would have been right to do so. He surrendered his trust and spoke before he could reason himself out of it. "I'm looking for someone who used to be an inquisitor."

Most reasonable people would have laughed. Angela did not. "I was under the impression one didn't leave that role."

"True enough for most. But he's something of a special case."

"You think he's the man you fought in the alley?"

Tomas shook his head. "They weren't the same size, nor did their skills match."

"You think I have two inquisitors in my town?" A note of disbelief crept into her voice.

"I think you have a former inquisitor and one current. I'm not sure they're connected."

"You really think they aren't? That would be one hell of a coincidence."

"True."

They made good time, their mounts eating up the distance between the town and where Tomas had fought the sniper. He pointed off to the side of the road, and they left the trail.

"I'm convinced that there's something happening in Razin," Angela said. The admission came out of nowhere, startling Tomas. "It's nothing specific I can put my finger on, and all my investigations have revealed nothing. But there's something."

"What do you mean?"

Angela looked like she regretted telling him as much. "It's small things. We find a surprising number of dead travelers within ten miles of the city. No one knows them, but they're all in terrible condition. It's like starving people randomly decide to make for Razin, but never make it." She grimaced. "Kids go missing from Ben's place more often than they should, too."

Tomas tensed. Had he been wrong about Olena? Or was she a victim, too?

Angela seemed to see into his thoughts. "It's not them. I was suspicious of the same, at first. But I'm convinced they're exactly who they say they are. Just two people, trying to help those kids. Maybe twice a year, though, a child goes missing. There's never any explanation except that they ran away, but Ben and Olena both swear the kids would never do such a thing."

She turned so she was facing him more directly. "That's why you telling me you saw Robick is such a big break. He loved it at Ben's place."

Tomas felt his mind twisting as he tried to fit everything together.

He grunted. "I have absolutely no idea what's going on."

"Well, that makes two of us."

They came to the approximate area, and Tomas began searching his memory to find the exact location. Despite that night being dark, he remembered the land well. The violence of that night had imprinted every detail on his memory, and time had yet to wash it away. It only took him a couple of minutes to find where he fought the sniper.

He slid off his horse.

There. "Right here," he called out to Angela. He hurried over, then came to a stop.

The grassland was empty.

Angela stood next to him. They stared at the spot together. There was plenty of evidence of the fight. The ground was still soaked in blood, and the grass had been trampled. But there was no body.

"I thought you said there weren't any scavengers around," Tomas said.

She shook her head. "Scavengers don't carry the entire body away."

Tomas swore. "Robick." In less than a heartbeat he was back on his horse, kicking it to a gallop. It only took seconds to cover the ground he'd crawled across a few nights earlier. He pulled the horse roughly to a stop and jumped off.

This was where he'd made his camp. Where Robick had met his end.

There was no body here, either. He swore, and a few

moments later, Angela rode up behind him. "Nothing?" she asked.

He shook his head.

She climbed down off her horse and studied the scene. Again, there was enough blood to confirm at least part of Tomas' story. Angela combed through the grass and found something else, too. Bone fragments.

"Probably from his skull," Tomas said. "Sniper got him in the back of the head."

Angela straightened up. "Who would go to all the trouble to find the bodies and then hide them from us? And why? I can understand the sniper. If he was someone I recognized, it would give me something to follow up on. But why Robick?"

Tomas just looked slowly around the grassland. He had all the same questions as Angela, but none of the answers.

It was during that slow turn, though, that he caught a brief glint of light far off in the distance.

His eyes went wide, and he jumped to tackle Angela just as a bullet split the air.

12

The first bullet zipped through the spot Tomas had stood a heartbeat before. The second, impossibly soon after, slammed into Tomas' back as he tackled Angela. He grunted as a fiery pain exploded in his right shoulder.

They hit the ground hard, and two more bullets followed them into the grass, dirt erupting in small geysers to Tomas' right.

Angela shoved him off her and rolled to her stomach. The rifle was in her hands before she noticed the blood staining his tunic. The bullet had passed through his shoulder but had altered its trajectory enough to keep her safe. She gave it a brief glance, then turned her attention to their assailants. "Must be two or three," she said. "You saw them?"

Tomas grimaced against the pain and nodded. He pointed in the direction he'd seen the glint of metal.

He almost reminded her to keep her head down, but there was no need. She kept low and moved away from Tomas. When she poked her head above the grass again, it would be in a different place.

It wouldn't be a poor idea for him to move, either. The snipers knew where he was.

Tomas took a deep breath. Elzeth burned within him.

Brighter than he should have.

"Elzeth?"

"You're pretty useless in a rifle battle in the prairie without your sword arm," the sagani replied.

Tomas couldn't make much argument there.

Recently, it had been Elzeth pushing the limits of their abilities. The sagani liked the loosening of the rules they'd set for themselves so many years ago. The threat of madness still worried Tomas. Only his trust of Elzeth kept pulling him forward.

The report of a rifle cracked the air again. Three shots, so quick together they almost sounded like one uninterrupted report. Tomas dove but didn't hear or see any bullets near him. He rolled over his good left shoulder and came to a crouch on his feet. He spun but couldn't see Angela.

Something about the shots bothered him. It tickled the edges of his awareness.

This wasn't what it seemed.

Did he search for Angela?

Distance was their friend and their enemy. Together, they could be more easily targeted by the snipers. But if she was injured, she would need his aid.

He kept moving away. His gut told him she was fine. That she hadn't been hit. Somehow, he couldn't imagine her falling here. Not like this.

His arm would still take a few minutes to heal. There was a very real chance this fight was over before he could even take part.

Even if he couldn't fight, he could still help.

"Going to need some strength," he said.

Elzeth burned brighter. Tomas felt the gentle wave of energy fill him. It deadened the pain. Made him ready for the fight ahead.

Tomas stood. Then he ran.

There was an art to not getting shot. Tomas shifted speeds frequently, going from a full sprint to a walk and back again. He changed angles. He embraced random movement.

With Elzeth's strength and speed, it made him nearly impossible to hit.

He wouldn't just distract the snipers. He would heal as he ran, and when he found himself among them, he would show them the superiority of his sword.

Tomas didn't hear the shot until after it punched him high in the chest, less than an inch from the healing shoulder wound. Too high to clip any vital organs, but it still felt like the world's strongest blacksmith had taken his hammer to Tomas' body.

The impact spun him around, and a second bullet, less than a heartbeat behind the first, scored a burning line across his abdomen.

He stumbled and tripped in the tall grass. The strength in his legs failed him as Elzeth focused everything on healing up his wounds.

Tomas squeezed his eyes shut against the pain, grinding his teeth together so as not to shout.

He was out of the fight, at least for a few minutes.

And in a few minutes, this fight might very well be over.

No one should have been able to hit him. He didn't believe it was hubris that spoke, but experience. Even if he granted someone a lucky first shot, the second had been far too close.

Not far away, another rifle boomed.

He wanted to shout at Angela, to warn her that something wasn't right.

The sniper responded in kind, a duel of thunder that rolled across the plains. Another two shots.

Angela didn't respond. Either she was dead, injured, or in hiding.

No matter. His task was the same.

Almost always two shots. Back-to-back, with barely a moment between them. Why would two snipers coordinate their shots in such a way?

They wouldn't.

The simple thought hit him almost as hard as the bullet had earlier. They didn't face a group of snipers, but one sniper with unnatural speed.

A host with a rifle.

Tomas swore.

No wonder he couldn't avoid the shots.

Angela was in even more trouble than he had thought. No matter her skill, she couldn't fight against such an enemy. Not out here.

Of course, he wasn't much good either.

Silence settled over the prairie. The air, once filled with the thunder of rifles, now carried only a soft breeze that rustled the tips of the grass above Tomas' head.

He didn't like not knowing.

Elzeth sharpened his senses in response to his unspoken wish. His healing slowed, but the wounds were mostly closed already. He heard Angela. Her heart pounded in her chest, but her breathing was smooth and even. Uninjured, then, and calm despite her fear.

He couldn't hear the other host. Too far away, likely, even for his hearing. If Tomas was a dishonorable, rifle-carrying sniper, he too wouldn't have neared. The distance between them was nearly as good as an impenetrable shield.

Tomas swore again. Were he a true fool, he'd get up as soon as he was strong enough and charge the sniper. But he strongly suspected he would have no better luck. He had an idea.

He just didn't like it.

It made him no better than the sniper shooting at him.

His shoulder burned, but they couldn't afford to wait. He crawled toward where he had heard Angela. With every foot he advanced, he expected bullets to rip through the grass around him.

None came.

When he thought he was close enough, he whispered, "It's me. Are you hit?"

"Just a scratch."

Tomas crawled the rest of the way to her.

Perhaps it was just a scratch, but it was across the side of her head and bleeding fiercely. The left side of her face was coated in dried blood. She'd been inches from dying.

"I need your rifle," he said.

She handed it to him without comment. He took it, surprised. He'd expected to have to convince her. "They're a host, too, aren't they?"

"Think so. Makes more sense than a group always firing at the same time."

She stared at his bloody tunic. "You sure you can even fire that?"

Tomas had been trying hard not to think about how unpleasant it would feel to put the butt of the rifle up against his injured shoulder. "Not well, but not much choice, either."

"What's your plan?"

"Spread out, maybe twenty, thirty paces apart. When I shout, you put your head above the grass, but only for a moment. Don't give them enough time to aim. I just want a second or two where their rifle isn't aimed my way."

"I can give you that."

"No heroics," he cautioned. "I shouldn't need long."

They crawled away in opposite directions, hugging the ground tight. The breeze made tracking them through the grass more difficult, but Tomas still expected a bullet with every breath he took.

He stopped and listened. Again, he heard Angela, breath steady even though her heart pounded. A remarkable woman.

"How am I?" he asked Elzeth.

"Shot. Twice."

Tomas rolled his eyes.

"You're probably not going to die."

"We're going to need everything."

"I know."

Tomas took a deep breath. He relaxed his body. "Now!" he shouted.

He heard Angela rise. He let his heart beat once, then he followed suit. As he came to his feet, Elzeth flared, brighter than the sun overhead. Tomas dropped his barriers, and thoughts faded. Movement, perhaps 150 yards away, caught his attention. A glint of metal as the barrel swung toward him.

He brought Angela's rifle up first. He lined up the sights and pulled the trigger.

A second bullet followed the first, shot as fast as he could pump the lever.

He didn't think he would hit his target. Shooting disgusted him, and he was no good at it.

But he could point it in roughly the right direction. And he could fill the air with lead.

With any luck, that would be good enough.

He pumped the lever again and again, keeping the sights roughly in line with his enemy.

Tomas made a statement.

Even if he fought a host, the host wouldn't dare full unity. Tomas was still faster, still dangerous.

When the rifle was empty, he waited for the host to respond.

13

The host retreated, firing as he did.

Tomas pursued, shifting left and right as the barrel tracked him. Bullets sped through the air, only missing him by inches.

When Tomas crested a small rise, he saw where the sniper had left his horse. Tomas ran faster, desperate to catch the man before it was too late.

The sniper didn't panic. The barrel of the rifle never strayed more than a bit from Tomas, and the host fired several times.

Tomas could only run between bullets for so long. One caught him in the left arm.

United with Elzeth, he barely noticed.

The sniper climbed on their horse with a smooth motion. They kicked the animal into a gallop, then twisted in the saddle to fire off several more shots. None came close to Tomas, but they brought him to a stop. Even he couldn't chase the sniper on horseback. Not for the distance that would be required.

The sniper rode south, never slowing.

Tomas let Elzeth fade. Brick by brick, he rebuilt the walls that kept them separate. As each mental brick was laid, the pain and exhaustion in his body built. By the time he was himself, he was firmly regretting the decision.

Angela approached, cautious at first, then faster when she saw the retreating form of the sniper.

He turned toward her and gave her a small wave. Even that made his legs wobble underneath him. "I'm just going to rest for a minute," he said.

His legs finally buckled, but he was unconscious before he hit the ground.

HE AWOKE in the same place he'd fallen. His eyes snapped open, and he saw that Angela remained. Sometime while he'd been out, she'd brought the horses over. She stared off in the distance.

"Thanks for not leaving me to walk all the way back," he said.

His voice startled her, and she flashed a quick, embarrassed grin.

"Thank you for taking a bullet for me."

Tomas searched his mind for a witty reply, but he was still tired. He settled for a quick nod.

"You always bring this much trouble into towns?"

"Seems that way, as of late."

She didn't answer for a moment, lost in her own thoughts. Then she gestured to his injuries. "Been watching those close up. Must be nice."

He ran his fingers over the bullet wounds. New, raw flesh had knitted over them. His shoulder and arm still burned while Elzeth healed underneath the skin. "Suppose it is. Nicer to not have to heal in the first place."

Questions danced in her eyes. The same questions everyone had about being a host. But she didn't ask them.

Tomas noticed he was a bit disappointed. He would have looked forward to answering her questions. He wanted her to be curious about him.

Her mind wasn't on him, though, but on the events surrounding Razin. "I don't even know how to start protecting my people," she admitted, speaking low as though she was revealing a terrible secret.

"You've got two inquisitors, one host, and at least one dead sniper from the Family in your town. People end up missing or dead far more often than they should, but you say it's always strangers you find in the prairie?"

He could see her running down the list of victims in her mind. "Always. You seeing Robick was the first time we've heard anything about someone I'd consider a citizen."

"You don't have any particularly mysterious people in your town, do you?"

Angela didn't dismiss the question out of hand. "We're growing, but I still feel like I know most everyone in Razin. And I pay particular attention to veterans. Hells, I try to notice anyone who looks like they know how to use a sword. As we keep growing, I'll probably deputize them."

He liked the way she thought of her work. She was proud, but not defensive. A rare combination.

Seemed hard to believe someone as competent as her would miss so many people. It was possible, but unlikely. "Maybe they aren't in town," he said. "Maybe they're just somewhere near."

She wanted to believe the explanation. It made her less culpable. Her eyes lit up for a moment, but then dulled as she shook her head. "There's nothing but farms for miles."

"You know them?"

Angela grimaced. "Not all, and not as well as I should. The people in the town take up most of my attention." She clenched her fists. "It's a lot of prairie to search."

They lapsed into silence again. Tomas would have liked to be a better help, but he was as lost as she was.

Not only that, but the encounter with the host had stolen most of his desire to help. When he'd spoken with Hadwyn's parents, he'd thought he was only going to be hunting down an inquisitor. That was something he'd do gladly.

But inquisitors certainly didn't work with hosts. And the church wouldn't work with Family. At least, they never had before.

Which made all this one confusing mess that he wanted no part of.

Angela interrupted his thoughts.

"I'd like your help," she said.

"You planning on deputizing me, too?" He couldn't quite keep the disbelief out of his voice.

"Somehow, I don't think you'd take too kindly to that." She took a long breath. "Whatever's happening is beyond me and my deputies. They're all plenty skilled for most of what needs to be done around town, but this is too much. I can't let this continue. I propose a partnership."

When he didn't immediately object, she kept talking, her words coming fast. "I'll help you find your inquisitor, and in exchange, you help me. I can't give you complete immunity, but I can look the other way for minor infractions."

She was so earnest about her offer. He kept the smile off his face. It had been a long time since he'd viewed the law as anything other than an annoyance he had to sometimes deal with. No doubt, she thought the offer extraordinarily generous.

"Deal," he said. He probably would have helped her anyway. At least this way, he got goodwill and maybe even some information in exchange.

She visibly relaxed. "Thank you." She glanced at the position of the sun. "You good to get back yet?"

"Almost," he said. "Another half hour or so and I should be able to move without ripping anything open."

Elzeth snorted. "You're fine."

Tomas ignored the sagani.

"So," Angela said, leaning back on her elbows, "why are you looking for a former inquisitor?"

"You're not one to let a question go, are you?"

Her grin was answer enough.

He looked around the grasslands. The land was green from plentiful rain. For as far as he could see, they were the only two around. And, he was surprised to find, he liked it that way.

"You should tell her," Elzeth said.

So, he did. "My body and mind aren't acting the way I think they should," he confessed.

He noticed the look she gave him. The same look any kind human gave to one with a terminal illness. He understood, but still, he hated that look. He didn't want her pity.

"Not that," he said. "The opposite, actually. Have you noticed any tics from me since we've met?"

She frowned, then shook her head.

He'd expected the answer, but her confirmation still came as a relief. Some days, after a full day alone in the frontier, he worried he was going mad, and that a symptom of his madness was an inability to recognize it.

"I've been a host, longer than most. Far longer. A couple

of months ago, I had to fight an enemy stronger than any I've fought before. I should be going mad, and yet I feel better than ever." He pointed to his wounds. "These are even healing faster than they should."

"And this inquisitor you're looking for can help?"

Tomas shrugged. "Maybe. He knows as much about the sagani as anyone I've ever met. If anyone has an idea, it'll be him."

"Unusual knowledge for an inquisitor."

"He was always unique. The church used him to investigate the sagani, to see how they might be killed."

"And he's going to help you?"

"I think he will. We have a history."

Angela stood up. "You're an interesting man, Tomas. I get the feeling you could tell some stories that would make even Callum's regulars shut up and take notice. Now let's get going."

It had been far less than a half hour.

She seemed to know his thoughts. The corner of her mouth turned up in a smile. "You're healthy enough to ride back to Razin, and I need to get back to town."

He almost continued with his bluff, but one look at her told him it wouldn't fly.

He conceded the point to her, and together they rode back to Razin, side by side.

14

The conversation flowed freely between Angela and Tomas on their ride back to Razin. A few minutes of fighting side by side had transformed them from relative strangers to allies.

Maybe even friends, though that wasn't a title Tomas granted lightly.

Tomas wasn't surprised.

Fighting, either against someone or beside them, was the quickest way to understand a person.

Combat stripped away pretenses, revealing the true self most people weren't even aware of. A three-minute sparring match told Tomas more about a person than he'd learn in three years of polite conversation.

He'd known, before being attacked, that Angela was curious. Now he also knew that she was courageous, trusting, and more than competent.

Razin was fortunate to have such a marshal.

He asked her how she'd gotten the job.

"Same way most marshals get the job," she said. "In

recognition for feats of bravery and an unquestioned devotion to duty."

"Take it that was the line on your orders?"

She nodded. "I understand why they do it, obviously. It gives soldiers something useful to do after the war. And they need loyalists out west to keep things from spiraling out of control. But sometimes it does feel a bit like being put out to pasture."

"Why did you do it?"

"Mostly wasn't sure what else I could do. I didn't have a lot of skills besides fighting, and I wasn't looking to get hitched. So, I accepted the orders and came out here."

As Razin came into view, she turned the conversation back toward him. "Tell me more about this inquisitor of yours. What does he look like?"

"Not much to distinguish him by," Tomas admitted. "He was the kind of man you would cross by on the street and barely even notice. Average height and weight. Brown eyes. No identifying marks or tattoos. When I knew him, he shaved his head, but I suspect that's no longer true."

"Why?"

"It was a sign of his devotion to the church. A personal vow. When he broke with the church, I imagine he let his hair grow in."

"What's his name?"

"Killan, though I'd assume he's changed it."

Angela glanced sideways at him. "So, your plan was to wander around town until you saw someone who looked familiar?"

"Pretty much."

He ignored her as she shook her head in disbelief.

A lone rider galloped their way from the edge of town. Elzeth flickered to life just long enough for Tomas' eyes to sharpen. He saw the red thread stitched above the man's heart. He didn't recognize the man, but Angela clearly did. She swore under her breath. "Best not to say anything, if you please," she told him.

Angela brought them to a stop, forcing the rider to have to come all the way to them. Tomas wondered what was so urgent the man needed to saddle a horse and gallop out of town to intercept the marshal.

A minute later the rider was before them. His face was red, and Tomas wasn't sure if it was because of the sun, the exertion, or rage.

The man pointed a stubby finger right in Angela's face. "How dare you," he proclaimed.

Angela didn't give him the benefit of a reaction. "Devon, this is Tomas. He's new to town. Tomas, this is Devon, a priest of the First Church of Holy Water and the leader of the local mission."

"You have one of your deputies watching the mission," Devon said. The way he spoke made it sound like Angela had burned their holy book. "It's an outrage!"

Angela sounded bored when she replied. "Perhaps you are unaware of the events in town recently?"

Somehow, Devon managed to puff out his chest even further than it had been. "Of course not. I'm well aware of the misfortune that has befallen poor young Hadwyn. But that is the very nature of my complaint! The presence of your deputy implies you believe there is some involvement on the part of the church."

Tomas considered mentioning the inquisition, just to see what kind of reaction he might get. Remembering Angela's request, though, he held his tongue.

"Not in the least," Angela replied. "But the description of the man who attempted to kidnap Hadwyn doesn't match anyone I know of in town. Right now, I believe a stranger is involved, and I have deputies watching all the places such a man might seek shelter."

"If that is all, you can dismiss your deputy," Devon argued. "I will tell you if any strangers seek shelter in the mission in the next few days."

"I appreciate that," Angela said, "but the deputy's presence is also for your own safety. Any man who would kidnap a child from their bed in the middle of the night is likely one who would have little respect for the church."

Devon harrumphed, and his eyes darted from side to side as he sought a new argument that might sway the marshal. He didn't appear to be finding any. He changed tactics. "Your dismissal of my concerns only reinforces my belief that you are not fit to be marshal! You can rest assured that the governor will hear of this flagrant breach of decorum!"

He turned his horse around and galloped back to town without giving her a chance to respond.

"A charmer," Tomas observed.

Angela snorted.

"Seems like trouble, pushing the church like that. Was he serious?"

"He was. Not the first time he's sent a letter of complaint to the governor."

"The governor backs you, even under pressure from the church?" If so, Angela must have been some sort of war hero.

She snorted again. "Not even a little. If good marshals weren't so hard to find, he'd have removed me long ago. Fortunately, everyone knows the railroad is coming, and he needs this town clean. Still, this might be the complaint that finally pushes him too far. The church and I don't get along too well, and they'd be happy to see me go."

"Any particular reason?"

"Mostly because I don't worship their god or the ground they walk on." She nudged her horse back into motion. "Come on, I still want to get back to town."

The ride didn't take much longer, but they didn't make it far into Razin before they were interrupted. Angela, it seemed, was a woman sought by all. A man, who Tomas recognized as one of Angela's deputies, stopped them barely a few houses in. "Ma'am, we found Ben."

Angela leaned forward in the saddle. "Where?"

The deputy gulped. "Sorry, I meant to say, Ben found us. He's been asking for you."

The deputy looked around, then lowered his voice, even though no one was near.

"He thinks his children are in danger."

15

Tomas followed Angela and her deputy to the jail. Neither objected to his company. They tied up their horses to the hitching post in front and hurried in. Another deputy sat in the office, and he pointed his thumb down the hallway and out the back.

Tomas hesitated. Curious as he was, this was still Angela's town. Ben hadn't asked to see him, and it seemed rude to assume Angela would want him by her side.

Angela put his concerns to rest. "Come on," she said as she gestured for him to follow. "You're as mixed up in this as anyone, and you were the last person to see Robick alive. Ben will want to meet you, too."

He hurried to catch up to her as she reached the exit. She opened the door and he blinked as he stepped from the darkness of the cells into the light of day.

A lone man stood there, his back to them. He looked up at the clouds, and Tomas had the impression that he was somehow seeking answers from the random shapes.

Ben turned, and his gaze met Tomas'.

Tomas froze in place. His jaw dropped, and he swore.

Everything made sudden, sickening sense.

Elzeth, tired from his efforts earlier in the day, was a second slow to react. He caught fire, but the other man was already in motion as Tomas reached for his sword. One moment, the man stood empty-handed, the next, he was leaping to his right, a familiar blade in his hand.

There were evenings when memories of that weapon haunted Tomas' nightmares.

Ben's leap meant Angela was no longer between them, and Tomas knew well enough what came next. Ben snapped his wrist, and the dagger flew at Tomas. Sunlight glinted off the thin chain that connected Ben to his favorite weapon.

Tomas shifted left, and the dagger missed.

Ben was already spinning, his motion whipping the dagger into a tightening spiral.

Tomas had come across a few warriors who thought themselves masters of the unusual weapon, but none of them could hold a candle to Ben's skill.

The blade whirled and snapped out at Tomas as though it had a will of its own.

In the tight confines of the training ground, there was little room to retreat. And Angela's presence complicated matters. Tomas tried to draw his sword but was forced to dodge before he could. He needed time and space, and Ben granted neither.

He knew Ben's skill. Knew what it would take to stop him, here, in this moment.

Elzeth was less certain. He understood Tomas' request, but twice in one day was unheard of. The sagani enjoyed testing their new strength, but this frightened even him.

Angela's life was worth the risk, though.

Tomas let the boundary between him and Elzeth

dissolve. Thoughts faded as instinct took over. Ben's dagger, once so fast Tomas could barely track it, slowed.

The dagger spun, and Tomas noticed how it was angled away from Angela. Then it snapped out at him again, faster than any snake.

Tomas leaned to the left. He didn't try to catch the dagger itself, recognizing the danger in the attempt. But he caught the chain just behind.

Ben was prepared. He twisted and pulled with his whole body.

Against unity, though, his strength was nothing.

Ben's eyes widened, realization setting in.

Ben wasn't a host, but at times, he almost acted like one. There was no deliberation, no hesitation in his actions. He dropped his chain, breaking the connection between him and Tomas. He advanced in quick, balanced strides, a dagger appearing in each hand.

The exchange was brief. Ben stabbed and slashed, both blades glinting as they caught the fading sun. He carved intricate and lethal patterns into the air between them. Tomas took the chain in his hand, pulled it toward him, then spun it around and whipped it at Ben.

Compared to Ben's artistry, Tomas' attack was ugly and crude.

But effective.

Ben had to respond, his patterns interrupted. The chain tangled around Ben's arm as he blocked, and Tomas pulled the other man off balance.

After that, Ben had no chance. Tomas drove fists into his opponent, staggering him.

Ben was tough, though. He stayed on his feet and looked for a chance to counter.

Tomas gave him none.

Another quick combination rocked him backward even farther. Ben still held the daggers, but Tomas wasn't sure the older man could even see straight. Before Ben could recover, he snapped a kick at Ben's head that crumpled him to the ground.

Tomas let Elzeth rest then. They'd pushed too hard, too often, but he didn't feel any different than before. He let out a small sigh of relief as he tied Ben's wrists in front of him with his own chain. The madness hadn't set in yet. At least not that he could tell.

He stood up and turned to Angela, who looked about as confused as he felt. "Are you hurt?" he asked.

She shook her head, her eyes traveling from Ben's unconscious figure to him. If not for the trust he'd built up over the past few days, he was sure she'd be attacking him now, too. Finally, her eyes settled on him. "What in the three hells just happened here? Why does Ben have weapons?"

He heard the betrayal in her voice. The hurt at what she witnessed.

He spoke slowly. "You know him as Ben, but I've met him before, a long time ago." He judged her reaction and decided it was safe to proceed.

"I know him as Killan, and before he came here to start a place for the children, he was an inquisitor."

16

Tomas squatted in the dust and dirt of the training grounds while he waited for Killan to wake up. Angela paced back and forth, eyes always returning to Killan's unconscious body.

She made no effort to hide her emotions. Anger and betrayal warred for dominance, and whenever her pacing brought her near Killan's limp form, Tomas worried she would start kicking him.

He left her to her own thoughts, because he was lost in his own. They weren't all about Killan, either. He looked down at his hands, steady as ever. He turned them over, but they were the same as they'd always been.

"Do you feel any different?" Tomas asked.

A pause, then, "No." Elzeth felt like he had more to say, but he remained silent.

"What's happening to us?"

Elzeth had no answer. Instead, he responded with a question of his own. "What if we have no limit?" Though no one else could hear the sagani, he still spoke in a whisper.

Tomas had considered the same, though Elzeth was the first to speak it.

He made his hands into fists. His thoughts seemed clear. His body was still. He didn't know what having tics felt like, but he was as certain as he could be he didn't possess any.

Tomas looked up from his hands when he heard Killan stir. The inquisitor came to quickly and glanced around. He took stock of the situation in a heartbeat.

He groaned and sat up, eyeing his bound wrists. Tomas hadn't bothered to remove the dagger, so if Killan chose, he could try attacking again with his hands bound together.

If he tried, Tomas would kill him.

Killan's gaze met Tomas', and he gave a slight nod. "I didn't think I would ever see you again."

Tomas grunted. His questions could wait.

Which was good, because Angela's patience had run out the moment Tomas knocked Killan out. She stomped toward Killan and hauled him to his feet, ignoring the danger she put herself in.

Tomas stood as well, ready if Killan decided to try something foolish.

But Killan didn't attack, and the dagger dangled freely from the short chain. Tomas breathed easier at that. The inquisitor would never have a better opportunity. If he wasn't taking it now, he likely wouldn't.

"Tomas told you?" Killan asked Angela.

"He told me your name is Killan, and that you used to be an inquisitor."

Killan's face twitched. "Name's Ben now, but the part about being an inquisitor is true enough."

Angela turned her back on Killan, and Tomas tensed. But Killan remained perfectly still as Angela paced. She spun around rapidly on a heel and faced Killan again. "Why did you attack Tomas?"

Killan snorted. "Look at him."

When Angela didn't react, Ben turned serious. "He's here to hurt the children at my place."

Tomas' anger caught him by surprise. His hand was on his sword, and he'd covered half the distance between them before he realized what he was doing. He stopped midstride. He growled, "You're the one causing the children harm."

Killan raised an eyebrow at the accusation. He turned to Angela.

Tomas noted she'd taken a few steps back from both of them. She looked ready to bring her rifle to bear, and he wasn't sure which of them she'd point it at.

"I'm sorry that I never told you about my past," Killan said to the marshal. "Hopefully, you can understand why I might not share it. But you know me. Would I ever hurt the children under my care?"

Doubt filled Angela's eyes, but she still shook her head. She turned her doubting gaze onto Tomas, and he felt his stomach twist.

He made no plea for his innocence. If his actions out on the prairie didn't convince her, nothing would. He kept his focus on Killan. "When I rescued Hadwyn, I fought an inquisitor. I knew it wasn't you, but the style was unmistakable. And now I learn that an inquisitor is watching the very children who keep disappearing. That can't be a coincidence, can it?"

Killan's lips twisted in a snarl. "I just encountered a host out on the prairie, not two days ago. Then I find one here. One who I know has done dirty work for coin. That can't be a coincidence, can it?" His words bitterly echoed Tomas'.

"A host with a rifle?" Angela asked.

Killan nodded once, never taking his eyes off Tomas.

"We came across the same host," Angela said. "Tomas took a bullet for me."

"Good of him," Killan said. But he took a step back and let his muscles relax.

Tomas didn't drop his guard, but he felt as though the threat of violence had passed.

"You fought an inquisitor in town?" Killan asked Tomas. He didn't wait for Tomas to answer. "Makes sense you'd suspect me, then."

Killan stepped close to Tomas, every move deliberate. He held his hands out, so the dagger barely swung as he approached. He stared into Tomas' eyes. "I swear to you that I have upheld our agreement. To the letter and spirit."

The two men stared at one another.

"I believe him," Elzeth said.

Tomas shook his head, and Killan smiled. "Hi, Elzeth," he said. He turned away. "You should trust your sagani. He's wiser than you by far."

Tomas swore, and Angela looked at him, confused. "Elzeth?"

Killan answered before Tomas. "The name of the sagani he hosts. A remarkable creature."

Tomas' fists tightened, but Elzeth's laughter stole any anger he might have had.

"About time I get some recognition," Elzeth said.

Tomas ignored the sagani. They still had the problem of Killan to solve. "Killan—"

"Ben, please," Killan interrupted.

Tomas shot him an angry stare. "Ben claims he has not harmed anyone since I saw him last. To the best of your knowledge, is this true?" he asked Angela. "Do you believe him?"

Angela thought for a moment, but her answer came faster than Tomas expected. "I do."

There was certainly a part of Tomas that just wanted to stab Killan through the heart and be done with it. But not without cause.

Tomas unwrapped the chain from around Ben's wrists and handed him the weapon. "Try something. Please."

Ben just smiled. He rolled up his sleeve and began the intricate process of concealing his weapon once again.

"Tell us what you know," Angela said.

Ben spoke while he worked. "A new girl arrived a few days ago. Ten years old, and on the brink of starvation when she found us. Said she'd come this way because she heard of a farm that offered food and shelter to all who wanted it."

"A farm?" Angela asked.

Ben nodded. "She was rather specific on that part, actually. She knew it was near Razin, but the rumors she'd heard told her not to come into town. If not for her extreme hunger, I don't think she would have." Ben finished with the weapon and pulled down his sleeve. "When I heard that, I decided to investigate."

"You should have come to me," Angela said.

Ben shrugged. "It was a slim lead to go on. No telling if a rumor means anything or not." He paused and looked at Tomas. "Anyway. If I'd found anything, I had planned on taking care of it myself."

Tomas snorted. Once an inquisitor, always an inquisitor.

Angela seemed content to overlook the implications. "What happened?"

"Like I said. I ran into a host with a rifle. Never got close enough to identify, though. Then I see Tomas here, and assume the worst. Didn't think he'd fallen far enough to use a rifle, but it's been quite a few years."

Angela looked between the two men. "You two really don't like each other, do you?"

"It's complicated," Ben said.

"He tortured me for four days straight," Tomas said.

"Like I said," Ben said. "Complicated."

Angela shook her head in disbelief, then returned to the matter she cared more about. "Did you find anything?" she asked Ben.

"No. I'd come across nothing suspicious before I ran into the host. But I'd been gone long enough, so I wanted to return and check on the children. And I hoped I could convince you to help. There're too many farms around for me to check on my own."

"Veric is injured," Angela said. "But not dead, thanks to Tomas. We're a bit short." She bit her lower lip. "I'll put two deputies on it while I keep an eye on town."

Ben offered her a deep bow. "Thank you."

Angela again looked between the two men. "If I leave you alone to talk with my deputies, you're not going to kill each other, are you?"

"We'll be fine," Tomas said, only half-believing his own claim.

Angela didn't look like she believed him, but she still went back into the jail, leaving the two men unaccompanied.

Movement at the corner of his eye caused Tomas to snap his head around.

But Ben wasn't attacking. Instead, he was bowing. He straightened. "You were the one who saved Veric and Hadwyn? I'd heard a concerned citizen helped."

"I was. Veric was giving me a hard time when we heard Hadwyn's parents cry for help."

"You've changed," Ben remarked. "The Tomas I knew

wouldn't have done such things. He certainly never would have saved a deputy."

"It has been several years. And you didn't catch me at the best point in my life. And in fairness, when I came searching for you, I never expected to find you running a shelter for orphans."

Ben acknowledged the point. "You were searching for me?"

"I was hoping you could help me."

"With what?"

Tomas gestured to one of the benches set up around the perimeter of the practice grounds. "Let's take a seat. I've got one hell of a story to tell you."

17

They sat side by side. Inquisitor and host. Water and Fire.

When their paths had last crossed, Killan had used every tool and technique at his disposal to coerce Tomas into talking. Tomas had sealed his lips, except for the screams. But Killan had been relentless, and Tomas had broken.

He'd learned something important about himself in those days.

This time, Tomas spoke freely, the words chasing one another in a rush to leave his lips. Ben sat and listened without saying a word.

Ben no longer served the Church of Holy Water, but the skills of an inquisitor would live on in him until the last beat of his heart. Tomas noted how Ben watched him, missing nothing. No doubt, he memorized every detail of Tomas' story as it was told, but that was only a fraction of what he learned from the tale.

Tomas finished by giving a brief recounting of events since he'd come to Razin.

Ben leaned back against the wall of the practice grounds and closed his eyes. "I'm glad that when our lives last intersected, it didn't kill you."

"Despite your best efforts."

Ben nodded, not debating the point.

"I'm not the only one who's been changed by the passing of years," Tomas said. "What happened to you?"

"The first year, after we parted ways, was a hard one for me. My departure from the church wasn't without conflict."

Tomas suspected that was an impressive understatement. Inquisitors didn't leave the church.

"By the time I was certain I was no longer being pursued, I'd come quite a ways west. Decided I liked the quiet, so continued west. Met Olena, and she changed everything for me, again. She wanted children, but I refused." The former inquisitor stared up at the sky. "My line ends with me. But I couldn't say no to her, and so we started the shelter."

"You don't have any connection to the church here?"

"Devon is an ignorant ass. Olena and I follow the old ways, and I stay well away from the church."

"You had no idea an inquisitor was in town?"

"None at all. As you can imagine, I'm possibly even more concerned by that than you are. Razin is the longest I've been in one place since we met, but I've planted roots here. The children need us." Ben scoffed at his own statement. "Well, really, they need Olena. I'm not actually sure I do much."

Tomas leaned back against the wall, too, matching Ben's pose. "So, you don't have any idea what an inquisitor, a Family sniper, and a host are doing in Razin?"

Ben didn't deny it immediately, but held up his hands when Tomas glared at him.

"Not specifically, no. But there's only one project they care about so much."

"The sagani?"

Ben nodded.

"How does any of this have to do with the sagani?"

"Don't know. I was never high enough up. Colvin, the gentleman you killed up in the mountains, he would have known."

"You know what he was?"

"They have no official name within the church structure. Their role isn't as defined as an inquisitor or a knight. But we all called them champions."

"You knew him?"

"Knew of him. Impressed you were able to kill him. Though you have gotten faster."

The comment brought Tomas back to the questions that had dragged him to Razin in the first place. "Do you have any idea what's happening to me?"

"I wish I did." Ben ran his eyes up and down Tomas slowly. "I've seen no sign of tics, though, and I think I've been observing you long enough I would have seen one. So, I'm inclined to believe your claim. You haven't noticed your thoughts changing? No sudden desire to kill and maim?"

"No more than usual." Tomas hesitated. "I do see ghosts sometimes. Men and women I served with."

"Does Elzeth see them?"

"Never."

Ben looked up into the sky, considering the question for a moment. "Of course, it's possible it's a sign of madness. But I'm more inclined to believe it's just a manifestation of the guilt you carry."

Tomas' protest died on his lips. Thanks to their time

together, Ben knew him too well. And, in a way, it was reassuring. "You don't think I'm going mad?"

Ben shrugged. "I don't think so, not from what I've seen today. But you've been a host longer than anyone I've ever met. And everyone goes mad. We know this. Still, it's been a long time since I've thought much about the sagani, and I try not to think of the time when I wasn't named Ben." He sighed. "Being as there's nothing here for me to do, I can return home and search through my notebooks. Maybe something will spark a memory that might help you."

Ben stood, and Tomas joined him.

Ben bowed deeply and rose. "It's a strange thing, standing here before you. You don't look like you've aged a day since I've seen you last. But I've always promised myself I'd say something to you if I ever saw you again."

Tomas narrowed his eyes.

"Thank you."

Ben bowed one more time, then met Tomas' gaze. "It was your act of mercy that allowed me to start a new life. You're the one who made my days with Olena possible." He looked like he wanted to say more, but he cut himself off.

He made to leave, but Tomas stopped him.

If they were offering confessions, he had one of his own.

"Those days changed us both," Tomas admitted. He bowed to Ben. "I was on a bad path, and our encounter straightened me out. Thank you."

Ben just laughed and shook his head. "Never thought I'd see us turn into old and sentimental fools."

"Speak for yourself. My best years are still ahead of me."

Ben grinned at that.

Behind them, Angela coughed loudly. They both spun around, surprised by her presence. "When I left you, I was sure you two were going to kill one another. Now, what, are you going to name your firstborns after each other?"

Ben laughed, but the moment faded quickly. "Angela, I'm sorry that I hid my past from you."

She waved his apology away. "I understand why you did. And if anything, knowing what you've accomplished, it makes you even more respectable."

"I wouldn't go that far," Tomas protested.

Angela returned to the business at hand. "I sent out the deputies I could spare. We'll investigate your rumor, Ben, and if anything comes from it, you'll be the first to know."

"Thanks," Ben said, "and I'll hold you to that. I want to be there when you go after Robick's killer."

With that, he was gone, leaving Tomas alone with Angela. She turned her inquisitive gaze toward him. "You going to tell me what happened between you two?"

"Now, or back then?"

"Both."

"Now, we agreed neither of us are responsible for what's happening."

"And back then?"

Tomas couldn't meet Angela's gaze. "After the war, I was in a bad place. Looking back on it now, I can understand, but I didn't then. I was a believer, and I was in one of the unnamed units for the back half."

Angela nodded. She'd served on the other side, so she knew well enough what Tomas had done. He was grateful not to have to explain it. It was, perhaps, one of the reasons he found Angela dominating his thoughts so often.

"When we surrendered, I didn't take it well. I made it my own personal war and fought on. Pushed the boundaries. Killan was smart, though, and caught me. Tortured me for four days."

"What was he searching for?"

"Everything. Information about being a host. Knowledge of things I'd done in the war. Plots and schemes I might have been a part of." Tomas shuddered at the memory. "On the third day, I realized he was looking for a way out. He had doubts. By the end of the fourth day, I'd convinced him to escape with me."

"You helped each other?"

"We did. It was a very bloody night. But we were both free, and it changed us both. My personal declaration of war ended the day I escaped. It was when I started wandering, and haven't stopped since."

"Have you ever considered settling in one place?"

He glanced over to her. Was that a hopeful note he heard in her voice, or did he just wish that was what he heard? He looked her in the eye. "Sometimes I do."

The corner of her lips turned up, the beginnings of a smile that she quickly hid.

She changed the subject. "What will you do now?"

"Return to Callum's. I need a full meal and some sleep. When your deputies find something, you know where to find me."

"There's a better inn, you know. One not filled with soldiers stuck in the past."

Tomas smiled. "And not spend the night in the very inn you recommended when we first met? I wouldn't dare."

18

E lzeth woke Tomas up. "Something's wrong."
Tomas came to full awareness in a moment.
Everything seemed as he remembered. He was in his room at Callum's inn. Below him, he heard impossible tales being met with loud cheers. That, combined with the pale red light of Tolkin pouring through his window, told him he hadn't been asleep for long.

A moment later the exhaustion of the past days hit him, confirming his lack of sleep.

He noticed nothing that concerned him. "What was it?" he asked.

"On the roof. Listen."

Tomas closed his eyes, immediately regretting it. The darkness behind his eyelids was welcoming, inviting him to return to sleep. He didn't hear anything.

He groaned and forced himself to sit up. If he remained horizontal for much longer, sleep was the only possible result. Elzeth wasn't one for false warnings.

The laughter from down below became even louder as a

story reached its climax. They drowned out any soft sounds Tomas might have heard. "Can you help me?"

Elzeth burned gently. Tomas ignored the crowd below him.

Then he heard what had worried Elzeth. The slight creak of a rafter as weight shifted on the roof above. Someone was perched up there. "Don't suppose it's just a coincidence, and they'll let me get back to sleep."

"Seems unlikely."

Tomas continued to listen.

Whoever was above him was disciplined. They didn't move much, but when they did, the roof responded with another soft creak. Just one person, though, and they didn't seem to be in a hurry to accomplish anything.

"What do you think they're up to?"

Before Elzeth could answer, the door to the inn opened. The familiar cadence of the stories faded into silence, and Tomas turned his attention below.

It took a moment, but with Elzeth's help, the sounds from the common room became sharp and clear. Tomas listened as though he were in the room. A fire crackled in the fireplace, warming the room against the chill of night. Callum's familiar voice greeted the new arrival.

"Welcome, traveler. Are you seeking food and shelter for the evening?"

There was a pause, too long for a natural lull in the conversation. Chairs scraped across the floor as Callum's other patrons prepared for quick movement.

Tomas twisted so he was sitting on the edge of the bed. While he listened, he put on his sword and boots.

"I have a problem, actually," replied a second voice. It wasn't one Tomas had heard before. "It concerns another guest at your fine establishment."

"The quiet guy?" another voice asked. "I knew he was up to no good."

"Indeed," replied the stranger. "He is up to no good, and there's a considerable bounty out east for him. I've come to collect."

More chairs scraped.

Tomas looked to the window. "What do you want to bet the person on the roof has a rifle, and is just waiting for us to sneak out?"

"The host?" Elzeth asked.

"It's where I would put them, if I was hunting myself."

"How much is the bounty?" asked one of Callum's patrons below.

"Sizable," answered the stranger, "and for good reason. He's very dangerous."

Bitter chuckles greeted that claim. "Didn't look like much to me," one patron said. A chorus of agreement echoed the sentiment. Tomas was offended by the lack of respect.

"Starting to think I'm not very intimidating," he said.

The stranger spoke again. By now, he had the attention of everyone in the common room. "Regardless, he isn't someone I would like to fight alone. Callum's inn has a reputation, far and wide, for providing shelter to some of the most skilled warriors west of the Tershall."

"Whole country," one drunk patron slurred.

"I would propose that for tonight, we work together. Help me capture or kill the man above, and I will share the bounty with everyone who helps."

"How much?" a patron asked.

"A hundred apiece." The answer came quickly.

If the common room had been paying attention before, the stranger was now the most important person in the world to the warriors below. A hundred, spent wisely, could last years. Spent poorly, it would still last several very memorable nights.

"How many people are down there?" Elzeth asked.

"Six or seven?" Tomas tried to remember. He'd been so tired when he returned, he hadn't paid as much attention to the common room as he usually did.

"Bounty on us wasn't that high when we crossed the Tershall."

Tomas had just completed the same math. "Not even close."

The number was too high, and even the mercenaries were doubtful. "You good for it?" one asked.

Tomas heard something heavy dropping onto a table. "Plenty more where this came from. Help me, and you'll all be paid by sunrise."

Given the lack of objections, Tomas guessed the stranger had proven his wealth.

"Callum?" one of the patrons asked. Apparently, the innkeeper was the last line of defense for Tomas.

The man didn't answer at first, and Tomas wondered if he would be moral enough to turn down the coin. No doubt, a fair amount of it would work its way into his pocket. "You say he's up to no good?"

"One of the most wanted criminals in the whole country. Done things that make me sick even thinking about."

"Capture or kill?" Callum asked.

"Capture would be best, but he's a fighter. If he dies, he dies."

"Fine by me, then. Be quiet on the way up. He's probably asleep by now, but best take no chances."

Several chairs scraped one last time as the patrons stood.

There were a few moments of organization as they prepared themselves for battle.

Tomas figured he only had a minute or two before they were at his door.

The window was always an option, but if the host was waiting above, his odds weren't as great as he would like them to be. He felt more comfortable fighting the six or seven drunk patrons.

More important, though, was the stranger who had hired them.

Tomas didn't believe someone had chased him here from out east. Not with that kind of money. This was about whatever was happening right here in Razin.

Which meant the man might have answers.

Tomas rolled his shoulders and stretched a bit to banish the last of the tiredness from his muscles.

"I take it we're staying?" Elzeth said.

"Be a shame not to greet our guests," Tomas answered.

The footsteps on the stairs were loud. Tomas grinned at their clumsy attempt at stealth.

Within a minute, they were outside his door, preparing to crash in all at once.

19

The key to Tomas' room scraped across the inside of the lock as one of Callum's patrons failed to unlock the door silently. In the otherwise quiet building, the sound was almost as loud as a gentle knock. Callum should have kept a few of his guests downstairs to start. The loud ones, capable of masking any other sound with their boasts and calls for more ale.

Tomas remained where he was, sitting on his bed. The mercenaries were close enough any movement might be heard. With Elzeth already burning, the few extra steps to the door didn't matter.

As the would-be intruders fumbled with the key for a moment more, Tomas idly wondered if Callum was among the mercenaries in the hallway.

As the key *thunked* loudly into place, Tomas decided the answer was no. Surely, if he was, he would have opened the door himself. No experienced innkeeper would struggle so mightily against a simple lock.

The lock surrendered to the clumsy assault, and the door began to open. First a crack, then wider.

Tomas attacked the moment he saw the first head poke all the way through the gap. In two steps he was close enough to aim a kick at the door. The head snapped around at the sound of footsteps, pale in the moonlight, eyes wide. Before the mercenary could shout a warning, Tomas' kick landed, right near the lock that had just posed so much trouble.

The door slammed into the first mercenary's head, smashing it between the door and the frame.

The unconscious body fell as the door rebounded, revealing the collection of greedy guests, hands full of weapons, outside his room. Most were advancing toward his door, but as he appeared, they instinctively paused, caught by surprise.

He'd been wrong about Callum. The innkeeper was near the back of the pack, looking more like a frightened mouse than the warrior of legend his stories made him out to be.

Tomas gave them no chance to regroup or organize. In the crowded hallway, he didn't bother drawing his sword. He laid into them with fist and elbows, Elzeth lending him a quickness none of them could match.

His elbow caught the first guest right in his nose. The man's head snapped back. Tomas used the same arm to punch another man in the stomach, doubling him over.

Neither were blows that would end the fight, but each moment the mercenaries spent concerned with their own pain was a moment he could focus on another warrior.

Their responses to his assault ranged from poor to tragic. Tomas twisted away from a poorly aimed stab, and the sword found another man's leg. One particularly large fellow swung a club at Tomas' head. When Tomas ducked below it, the club continued on its way, crashing into the skulls of two other mercenaries.

The whole attack was a farce.

It wasn't that his opponents were unskilled. But they were drunk, surprised, and overconfident. Against a host warned of their arrival, they had no chance.

Most of the fight was over within a minute. Blood pooled on the floor from three or four minor injuries, but Tomas didn't think any of them were lethal. He kicked at a couple of the mercenaries who looked more eager than the others to get up and try again.

When he was done, he found himself alone in the hallway with a woman and Callum.

The innkeeper somehow managed to look like he was cowering in a corner while standing in the middle of a hallway. Tomas ignored him. Callum could wait until he was finished with the other.

The woman was one of Callum's patrons. Tomas had noted her before. She had seemed calm and possessed down in the common room. Welcomed to the nightly party, but still somehow apart. That separation between her and the others was even more stark now. She had a knife in her left hand, the tip perfectly steady. If she had been drinking before coming up here, Tomas couldn't tell.

She looked down at her companions with disdain. "Figured you were tougher than they thought, but I didn't think it would be quite so one-sided." Her eyes traveled up to him. "You're faster than anyone I've ever seen before."

The accusation was there, unspoken. Perhaps she wasn't sure, but she had a pretty good guess as to what he was.

She lowered herself into a fighting stance. Even if she guessed, it didn't bother her. A smile played on the corners of her lips. "Suppose that's why you're worth so much, eh?"

Tomas didn't answer. He wasn't ignoring her, but the focus of his attention was on other sounds in the building, revealed by Elzeth's sharpening of his senses. Someone was marching around downstairs, moving with a purpose Tomas couldn't discern from sound alone. The stranger with the deep pockets, he assumed. And up on the roof, the host waited, as patient as ever.

His stillness caused the woman to attack.

Tomas backed up a few steps, dancing among the unconscious bodies of her companions. Tomas had the upper hand. The extra quickness granted to him by Elzeth allowed him to navigate the uneven terrain with greater ease.

She was good, though. Despite the bodies and the blood-slick floor, her footwork was nearly flawless. Her strikes, when they came, were as quick as any snake, her knife darting for his vitals.

Tomas evaded the cuts but saw no easy opportunity to strike back.

Then a thick and meaty hand wrapped around one of his ankles. He glanced down and saw the giant man who'd once wielded the club wasn't as unconscious as Tomas would have liked.

Tomas cursed as his retreat was halted. The woman's smile grew.

Getting out of the grip wouldn't be that hard. Getting out of it while the woman tried to cut him open would be nearly impossible.

The woman moved in, her knife darting, its final target almost unpredictable.

Elzeth burned brighter.

Unable to escape, Tomas blocked her next cut with his left arm. Her knife cut deep through his forearm, but she was cautious, dancing away before he could fight back. Below him, the grip on his ankle was growing stronger as the giant's senses returned. Before long, the giant would be struggling to his feet.

The woman attacked. Tomas took another deep cut to his left arm as he blocked her strike. Blood dripped down his arm, and again she danced back as he sought to counter.

Before he could think about kicking free of the giant's hand, she launched herself at him again.

He was tired of this. He lunged toward her as she advanced, catching her by surprise. The move was made awkward by the giant's vice-like grip, but he succeeded in throwing off her timing.

It cost him another deep gash along his arm, but he grabbed hold of her. He pulled with all the strength Elzeth gave him, tossing her behind him several feet.

She recovered quickly, but Tomas had given himself enough time to kick himself free of the giant. A boot to the man's face ensured he wouldn't bother Tomas again.

He was about to take the fight to her when he smelled something on the air. He sniffed, and this time the scent was far more powerful.

Smoke stung his nostrils.

He turned around to see flames flickering on the staircase below.

They grew too quickly to be natural, and soon smoke billowed overhead. Tomas crouched down so that he might breathe easier. He could already feel the heat.

The stranger had trapped them all up here to burn.

20

T he woman, distracted by the smoke, allowed Tomas enough time to bring his hand to his sword.

It signaled the end of the fight.

Her eyes darted to his hand, then back to his face.

She knew it, but she still considered attacking.

"I could kill you here," Tomas said. "Or we could both survive to enjoy another day."

For a long moment, Tomas thought she would still charge. Then she sighed. Her knife spun quickly in her hand, finding a home in a hidden sheath at her waist.

Tomas removed his hand from his sword and looked up and down the hallway. The flame had climbed further up the stairs. Callum ran toward it, seeking to flee. But he turned back before he even reached the top stair. The heat was too great.

Several of Callum's patrons were stirring, but two, including the giant, were nearly as still as the dead. Tomas swore and clenched his fist. Blood from his arm dripped down onto the floor.

The whole building groaned as though it were an injured warrior.

He couldn't hear if anyone was up on the roof still. Not that it much mattered. There was only one way out of the building.

Tomas turned to the woman. "Will you help me get them out?"

She stared at him as if he had lost his sanity. "No." She made her way to his room.

"There's a sniper out there, looking for me."

She stopped at that, then turned and stared at him.

"You might not want to be the first one out the window."

She looked to the fire, then the smoke gathering over their heads. She decided quickly. "Fine." She rejoined him in the hallway. "Good way to get more drinks out of them, anyway."

"Callum! Get over here!" Tomas shouted.

The innkeeper jumped, then obeyed. He wilted under Tomas' glare. "Yes?"

"Help us wake everyone up."

"How?"

"I don't know. Slap them." Callum paled at the idea. Tomas turned his attention to the woman. "Tie my sheets together to make a rope."

She nodded, and the two went to work.

Tomas focused on the window. The roof would soon be too hot to stand on, and who knew how long the building would last? If their roles were reversed, Tomas figured he would move positions. He crawled over to the window and pushed it open.

Nothing happened, and Tomas breathed a sigh of relief. Maybe his assailants considered the fire deadly enough.

Regardless, he kept himself out of sight.

A crowd was once again beginning to gather at his door, but they were far less hostile this time.

The woman had knotted two sheets together. It wasn't much, but Tomas' room was only on the second floor. If the mercenaries were healthy enough to attack him, they could survive a short drop. Four mercenaries looked ready to go. Callum was slapping the giant, but to no avail.

"If you can jump, jump," Tomas said. "Otherwise grab onto one end of the sheet and get down as fast as you can."

One of the mercenaries didn't need to be told twice. He ran to the window and looked down. He took a step back, and just as he was about to leap, his chest exploded.

The report of the rifle followed a moment later.

Tomas swore. "Other side. Quick."

They ran across the hall. The door to the room was locked, but it caved quickly to the combined efforts of the mercenaries and Tomas. The room was dark and empty.

Tomas ran to the window and pressed himself to the side. He opened it and peered out. He saw nothing that alarmed him, so he risked exposing himself. Nothing happened.

The mercenaries watched, and when he didn't get shot, began their evacuation. Two jumped out the window, while one used the rope the woman had made. One more mercenary joined them, staggering as though drunk. One of the two stubbornly unconscious fighters. Tomas tied the sheets around him and helped the woman lower him.

Callum entered the room. "I can't get Henk to wake!"

"Get out of here," Tomas said. Callum also used the rope, with the woman serving as the anchor.

Tomas went out to the hallway, forced to crouch nearly all the way down to avoid suffocation.

Henk, the giant, was still out.

Behind him, there was another gunshot. The woman came out of the room, bleeding from a cut on her arm. "Sniper moved."

"Callum?"

"Safe enough."

"Back to my room, then."

Tomas threw Henk's arm over his shoulder and lifted the man up. "Tie the rope around his waist." The woman did so, and Tomas swore when he saw how little was left after being wrapped around the enormous waist.

The woman took Henk's other arm, and together they walked him toward Tomas' window. Tomas' eyes watered as the smoke stung them. He wrapped the rope around his waist, grimacing as pain shot up his left arm.

They shoved the giant out the window.

If not for Elzeth, Tomas would have been pulled right out the window behind him. As it was, Tomas pressed one leg against the wall and barely stopped himself.

Henk hung, suspended a solid six feet above the street. The woman grinned at Tomas. "Well, looks like you have everything taken care of here." Without giving him a chance to reply, she jumped from the window, landing with a roll on the street below. She blew him a kiss and ran off.

Tomas' muscles strained against Henk's weight. He tried to lower the man gently, but he didn't have much time left. Smoke filled the air, filling his lungs and choking him.

He dropped Henk, then jumped out the window himself. As he did, a bullet shattered the window beside him.

Surprised, Tomas hit the ground harder than he intended. He rolled to his feet and ran. Above him, he heard footsteps sprinting across the roof.

He turned right at the first intersection, but the sniper

followed easily. The range of their weapon combined with the high ground made them even more formidable than before. Tomas ran faster as he approached an intersection. He dashed through as bullets tore up the dirt around him. One shot shattered the corner of a house, sending splinters toward Tomas' face.

He lifted his hand, and several of the splinters embedded in his hand and arm. Two cuts opened on his cheek. He ignored the pain and turned another corner. The footsteps pounded on the roofs behind him.

Tomas neared the edge of town and turned again. From up high he would be an easy target if he left the cover of the buildings.

Up ahead, barrels had been stacked close to a low roof. Tomas pushed harder, leaping up the barrels and onto the roof. The sniper greeted his arrival with a barrage. Had Tomas paused, even for a moment, at least one or two would have taken him in the chest.

The sniper tracked him too smoothly, though.

Fast as he was, he couldn't dodge a host with a rifle. When he saw the sniper's finger tighten on the trigger, he dove. A bullet ripped through the air above him and he crashed to the ground. He rolled, expecting another shot as he was prone. But it never came.

Tomas came to his feet and realized he was alone on the roof. A look around revealed nothing. He listened and heard feet running away down the street and the unmistakable sound of the rifle being reloaded. He began to give chase, then heard steel clash against steel in a different direction.

Towards Ben's place.

Tomas sprinted and leaped off the roof, landing, rolling, and returning to his feet. In less than a minute he was at Ben's, and the fight was already over. Ben rested against the wall of his place, chain and dagger on the ground. Three other bodies lay in the street.

When Ben saw it was Tomas, he waved him away. "Too much fighting for an older man," he said. "But I'm fine. I'm more worried about the marshal."

Tomas nodded, following Ben's thoughts. Someone was trying to tie up loose ends. "Sure you're good? Can't have you dying on me yet."

"Go."

Tomas did, running toward the jail.

The sound of the rifle ahead told him he was already too late.

21

Tomas ran as fast as his sagani-aided legs could carry him. Though he didn't dare risk full unity, he still covered the distance in less than two minutes, his long, quick stride bringing him ever closer to Angela.

He slid to a stop at the corner of a street that led to the jail. Using a shop for cover, Tomas poked his head out.

On every previous visit, the street had been quiet, empty except for a handful of customers browsing shops like the one he now hid behind. Under Tolkin's pale red light, it was transformed into a battlefield. Tomas saw two bodies on the street.

Two rifles fired, so close together they almost sounded like one mighty gunshot. Flashes of muzzles on rooftops across the street from the jail revealed the assailants' locations.

There was a flash from inside the jail. A lone rifle answered the assault, the sound quieter than either of the others. Tomas imagined Angela in her office, deafened by the report of her own rifle as she fought for her life.

Shadows gathered near the office, heading toward the back.

The rifles, then, were likely a diversion. As Angela focused on the snipers, the others would climb over the wall of the practice grounds and assault her position from the rear. If she was firing her rifle inside, she might not even hear them if they broke down the door.

Neither the rifles nor the assault was to be taken lightly.

Tomas crossed the street far out of sight of the rifles on the roofs. His steps were soft and swift as he ran to intercept the shadows.

He made one wrong turn that led him to a dead end. His memory of the town was imperfect, and he cursed himself for not understanding his battlefield better.

The delay only cost him a few seconds. He backtracked and ran to the next alley. Though he'd never seen them from this side, the familiar walls of the practice ground were easily recognizable.

No shadows stood outside the walls. They'd clambered over quickly.

Tomas ran for the wall, leaping and placing one foot about as high as his waist. Planting his foot allowed him to convert his sprint into vertical momentum. He grabbed the top lip of the wall with both hands and pulled himself up and over.

The shadows were gathered near the rear entrance, about to open the door.

Tomas' arrival diverted them from their intention. He landed and rolled, coming to his feet as he drew his blade.

There were four of them, and they charged him as a group.

Tomas cut the first man to reach him across the stomach. His enemy's sword was half a heartbeat too slow.

He pushed hard off his left foot, avoiding the overhand cut that hoped to split his head in two. Tomas cut across, leaving another dying warrior behind him.

The third warrior's attack was more balanced. Her sword sought his flesh, but he shifted away, always a breath ahead. When his opening appeared, he cut her down.

The final shadow realized his situation and retreated from Tomas. But it was too late. He'd locked himself in a practice ground that had become a killing field. When his retreat caused him to collide with a bench, his eyes went wide, but only for a moment.

Being backed into a corner was just the dose of courage the man needed. He lunged for Tomas, a desperate and clumsy attempt. Tomas easily twisted away and brought the hilt of his sword down hard on the man's head. His eyes rolled up in their sockets as he fell.

Tomas cleaned and sheathed his sword.

They'd been skilled enough, he supposed. Nothing special, though.

Only with his fight finished did he realize the gunfire from the front of the building had stopped. He approached the rear door cautiously. After a moment of debate, he knocked loudly on the door.

Nearly a minute later, the door cracked open, and the barrel of a rifle emerged. When Angela saw him, she let the barrel drop. "You frightened me," she said. Then she saw the bodies in the practice ground. "Ah."

"What happened out front?"

"I got one of them. The other retreated."

Tomas pointed at the last warrior he'd fought. "Left him alive. Want to open a cell for him?"

"Sure."

Considering the fight she'd just been through, Tomas

was surprised by how quick Angela's mind was working. She'd definitely been a hell of an officer.

She unlocked the cell while Tomas dragged the unconscious warrior into it. Once he was secured, Tomas studied Angela. "You hurt?"

"A few scratches from shrapnel, but nothing to worry about." She sniffed the air. "Why do you smell like smoke?"

"It's been an exciting night." He recounted his adventures.

When he was done, she grabbed a lantern and brought it out to the practice grounds. She examined the bodies. Each had the tattoos that marked them as Family.

Angela squatted next to the last body she examined and bit her lower lip. "The Family has no love for marshals, but this isn't like them. Too much trouble, by far."

Tomas looked up at the horizon, where Shen was just rising. "You don't have any idea what they're after?"

Angela stood. "Almost all the crime around here that isn't your usual petty trash has to do with the trade routes. There's a lot of money to be made. That might explain the Family's involvement, but it doesn't explain the inquisitor, or Hadwyn's kidnapping."

"Maybe they're unrelated?"

"Possibly." Her head snapped up. "You said Ben was attacked. Let's go to him."

Elzeth settled back into a slumber as Tomas and Angela ran from her office to Ben's place. As he did, Tomas' limbs grew heavy, and his thoughts slowed. He'd intended to rest this night, and instead had done everything but. Elzeth could mask many things, but eventually, Tomas' body had to pay the price.

He kept up with Angela, though, and they reached Ben's place in short order. Ben was no longer seated against the wall, which eased Tomas' concerns. The bodies remained in the street.

Angela examined them quickly. "No tattoos," she said.

Tomas leaned forward so that he might see. She'd spoken true, of course. "If they weren't Family, who were they?"

"Perhaps Ben knows."

They knocked on the gate to Ben's place, and he answered it so quickly Tomas suspected he'd been waiting on the other side. Ben shuffled out and closed the gate gently behind him. "Olena's awake, and she kept the children inside during the excitement. A few of the heavy sleepers didn't even wake." He looked to the bodies. "I'd rather the children not have to see that."

"We'll move the bodies before we leave. Any idea who they were?" Angela asked.

Ben's eyes darted from side to side, but he didn't immediately answer.

"You have a suspicion," Tomas said.

Ben nodded. "I have no proof, but I believe they were from the church."

"Knights?" Angela inserted an impressive amount of skepticism into one word.

"No, definitely not knights. Just believers."

Angela looked far from convinced, but Tomas didn't think Ben was lying. Whether he was right was another matter, but Tomas didn't take Ben's guess lightly.

"Do you need anything else?" Angela asked.

"No. We'll be fine. I'll keep watch tonight, but perhaps you'd spare a deputy or two to keep an eye on it tomorrow while I rest."

"First you want me to assign deputies to search the surrounding areas, now this? I'm running out of deputies."

Ben gave them a tired grin. "Good thing you've got him, then." He gestured to Tomas. "Though he looks like he needs a nap."

Tomas was too tired to retort.

Angela bid Ben a good night, then told Tomas to rest while she found a hand cart. She returned a few minutes later, and together they hauled the bodies onto the cart. They wheeled the corpses out of town, where Angela dumped them without ceremony several hundred feet off the main road.

"That's it?" Tomas asked.

"Good enough," Angela said. "They'll get no respect from me, attacking a place that houses so many children. I don't recognize them, so there's nothing more they can tell me."

Tomas bent over the bodies and said the old words.

From the One we became many.
  To the One we return.
  May the gates beyond
  Welcome your weary souls.

Angela let him say the old words without interruption, and he couldn't read the expression on her face when he turned his attention back to her. "You really believe, don't you?"

"I think so."

She smiled at that. After a moment of thought she said, "Come on. I've got too much work to do to rest, but the least I can do for you always saving my life is give you somewhere to sleep. You can rest at my place tonight."

22

Tomas woke the next morning in a bed far softer than any in Callum's former inn. Far softer than any he'd really known. From his upbringing in the sword school, where a bed was considered a weakness, to the military, where a proper bed was seen as an unnecessary expense and burden, he'd not slept in too many pleasant places.

Angela's place was near the top of a very short list.

He couldn't help but think that the only thing that could have made it better was Angela herself.

She'd escorted him to her home and made sure he was properly bandaged. Then he'd fallen asleep as she cleaned up after the chaos of the attack.

She'd come back very late, or very early, depending on one's perspective. Elzeth had woken him, but Tomas had been too tired to even stir.

For a full minute, she'd stood at the door of her bedroom, watching him.

Eventually, she turned around and slept on the couch.

He wished she'd chosen differently.

He stretched as he listened to the sounds of her in the kitchen. Her smell permeated the bed, and he let himself relax.

His worries were distant, at least for the moment. His sword was propped in the corner of the room, and for once, he felt no immediate urge to go tie it to his hip.

The demands of nature, and the increasingly powerful smell of breakfast, finally got him to roll out of bed. He looked out the window and the sun was lower on the horizon than he would have guessed. He supposed today wasn't really an ideal day for sleeping in. Angela's duties would consume most of her day.

He answered nature's call and made himself presentable. By the time he reached the kitchen, it looked as though Angela was nearly done cooking. She already wore her badge. "Morning," she said, flipping a pancake with a deft flick of her wrist. "Wasn't sure if you were going to wake up."

"Smelled too good not to."

She slid the pancake onto a plate and gestured to a small table. Two places were set, and Tomas took one. She sat across from him, and together they broke their fast.

"This is amazing," he said. And it was. Like fine beds, excellent meals weren't a great part of his life. Mostly it was trail food and cheap fare at inns.

"After eating Callum's gruel for a few days, I would imagine." She leaned back in her chair. "What will you do today?"

Tomas considered for a moment. Dozens of questions about last night's attacks plagued his thoughts, but he saw no quick path to answers. Any investigation he launched could be done more effectively by Angela. He considered offering his services to interrogate the Family assassin they'd caught, but even that was a task better left for Angela and her deputies. "I think I'll go visit Ben."

Angela nodded, her gaze focused. "If you discover anything, let me know."

"What about you?"

"There's still more to clean up from last night. I'll try the Family in the cell again, but he's not talking. I didn't recognize any of the attackers, so they haven't been in town much, if at all. I'll get a description of the man who hired the mercenaries at Callum's, but I suspect it'll just be another stranger."

Tomas didn't bother with empty platitudes. He didn't feel any closer to solving the mysteries of Razin than he did right after Robick was shot. "If you need me for anything, just ask. I'm happy to help."

To prove his point, he picked up their empty dishes and brought them to the sink. He felt her eyes on his back.

"You're welcome to stay here again tonight," she said.

His heart pounded a little harder. He put the dishes away, then turned to her. He offered a quick, short bow and a smile. "Thank you. I'd like that very much."

Since the moment he'd come into the kitchen, he'd felt like he was sharing the room with the marshal of Razin. Now she returned his smile, and he couldn't think of her as the marshal. She was only Angela. "Good. I would, too."

Then the mask of the marshal slipped over her face, and she stood. "Would you mind leaving through the back way?"

He couldn't help but laugh at that. "Too many jealous suitors?"

The look on her face told him he'd been more right than he knew. "You have no idea."

"That's not a problem," he reassured her.

"Thank you." She looked like she might say something

more, but then thought better of it. She strapped on her sword and slung the rifle over her shoulder. Then she was gone, leaving him alone in her house.

He considered looking around, but it felt inappropriate. He returned to the bedroom, armed himself, then left out the back way, making sure he was unobserved.

Eventually, he returned to the street, feeling the changes in Razin. By now, everyone knew what had happened. Unanswered questions would lead to quiet whispers. Doubts and fears would creep in as good citizens wondered if their families were safe.

Keeping the peace meant far more than just locking up the criminals. It meant answering questions, listening to complaints, and being a calm and stable presence in the midst of chaos.

All reasons why there were far more terrible marshals than good. Most marshals Tomas had come across were good enough with a sword. But they lacked all the rest.

He kept his head down as he crossed town to reach Ben's place. No one stopped him with any questions, and before long he found himself in front of the locked gate. The sounds of children at play cascaded over the walls, though, promising a return to normality. Tomas knocked on the gate and was let in by Olena. She welcomed him and told him Ben was inside. She locked the gate again behind him.

The yard was exactly as he remembered it, filled with children at play. He saw no concern over the locked gate, the burden of outside events borne by Ben and Olena alone. As he walked toward the house, Tomas caught a ball, an errant kick from a young boy. With a smile, he tossed the ball back and the children resumed their game.

A girl ran up to him and bowed. "My name is Clara. Welcome to my home."

Tomas gave her a smile. "Thank you, Clara. My name is Tomas."

The girl launched right into the reason for her welcome. "None of my friends want to have a tea party. Do you want to join me?"

Tomas laughed. "I'm afraid I can't now, but if I ever can, I'd love to."

Clara was obviously disappointed, but she held her head high. "I'll hold you to that promise," she said as she walked away.

Ben met him at the door. He'd watched the whole exchange. "A precocious child, that one." He let Tomas in, and together the two made their way silently to the dining room, where they sat across from each other.

"I fear for them," Ben said. "It feels like a storm building, just over the horizon. And they are the ones who will be caught out in the open when the hail starts to fall, and the wind picks up whole trees."

"They have you and Olena. More shelter than they would have had otherwise. And I'll help you stop them. Whatever's happening, it ends now."

Ben accepted the promise with a nod.

"Do you have any idea where they might be? Angela's deputies won't be able to search, at least for a few days. She'll want them here."

Ben shook his head. "I'm sure they're within a few miles of town, at the most, but beyond that, I couldn't say."

"It's got to be a good-sized place. Angela still hasn't recognized anyone, and there's been at least a half-dozen bodies. Plus the ones we haven't captured. A small farm-house wouldn't be big enough."

"That many?" Ben's features had suddenly grown sharp again.

Tomas nodded.

A pleased grin spread across Ben's face.

"I know how to find them," he said. He outlined his idea, and once mentioned, it seemed so obvious Tomas was bothered he hadn't thought of it first.

Tomas stood, ready to pursue Ben's idea immediately. Ben also pushed himself up from the table. His movements were slow. Tomas narrowed his eyes. Ben waved away his concern. "Not used to so much action," he said. He walked Tomas to the front door but didn't let him leave without a word of caution.

"You know the church is neck-deep in whatever is happening," Ben said. "Please be wary. There's always layers to everything they do, and I still don't think we've seen the depths they're willing to sink to."

"I'll be careful."

"You better be," Ben said with a wink. "It would be a shame if I had to save you a second time."

23

Tomas stood outside the general store, wondering once more if he'd made the right choice in coming here alone. Ben's final words had crawled under his skin, worming their way deep into his stomach, pulling it into a knot.

He'd crossed blades with the church a few times. For a group that proclaimed to carry the light into the darkness, they preferred to work in the shadows. Everyone knew the church was powerful, but few understood just how deep their roots extended. They preferred it that way. For all their scheming, they were rarely disruptive.

Their actions in Razin were too aggressive.

He should get Angela. She'd know how to approach the situation.

But she had at least a dozen problems competing for her attention. And it was just a general store. Hardly a place to fear.

He pushed the door open before he could talk himself out of it.

And immediately regretted his choice.

A giant stood behind the counter, his chest as wide as a cannon. When he spoke, his voice boomed like one, too. "Greetings!"

Tomas couldn't see the man's lips move. He had an enormous mess of facial hair, a full beard that covered the whole bottom half of his face and stretched down low enough that Ben's children could swing from it.

Tomas gave a small bow and began. "My name is Tomas and I—"

"I know who you are!" the giant interrupted. "We all do! The man who saved Hadwyn. Whatever you need, you will find Yanric offers you the best deals, on account of your heroism."

Tomas wasn't quite sure what to say. "Thanks. But I actually came here because I had a question I hoped you might answer."

Yanric frowned but shrugged. "An odd request."

"Angela and I believe that all these attacks in town are coming from someplace outside Razin. We think they are all hiding in a farm somewhere."

"No one in Razin would do what these scum have done," Yanric agreed.

"It occurred to me that such a group would have need for supplies," Tomas said, claiming credit for Ben's idea. "Has there been anyone in here purchasing more supplies than normal, or anything suspicious?"

Yanric thought for a moment, then shook his head. "Nothing comes to mind." He pulled out a ledger from behind the counter and opened it. He flipped page after page over, running his finger down the column of figures. Elzeth burned gently, allowing Tomas to run his own eye down the figures.

Yanric's claim was supported by the ledger. None of the

numbers were terribly large. Not enough to supply the number of people Tomas imagined.

Tomas swallowed hard as he considered his next question carefully. "I don't suppose there's anyone not in the ledger? People you simply have promises with?"

Yanric stood up to his full height. Tomas didn't think the man would attack, but it had definitely been the wrong question. "If it comes through my store, it's in the ledger," he said.

"Right." Tomas didn't press the issue, and besides, he believed Yanric. The man oozed pride in his town. He didn't seem the type to help the church tear it down. "Well, thank you, once again. If someone does try to make a large purchase, would you let Angela know?"

"Of course." The tone of the man's answer didn't encourage further questioning.

Tomas bowed again, thanked the proprietor profusely, and made a hasty exit.

"Everywhere we go, you're always making friends," Elzeth remarked.

"Had to be asked."

He walked far enough away from the store so as not to irritate Yanric further with his presence, then found a bench to sit on and stare up at the clouds as they raced across the sky. "Thought Ben's idea was foolproof," he admitted.

"His point remains," Elzeth argued. "Whatever's happening involves quite a few people. They've got to be getting supplies from somewhere."

"Another town?"

"There isn't one for a long way. I feel like it has to be here."

Tomas chewed on the problem. Setting up here wasn't

random. If the church was putting this many resources into something, nothing was accidental.

So why Razin? It was a good-sized town, but there were plenty of towns springing up like weeds across the frontier. There had to be something more. He grunted when he realized. "The trade routes."

"What?" Elzeth asked.

"The reason why Yanric doesn't have them in his ledgers is because the goods aren't being sent through his store. They're getting directly supplied by the traders."

After a moment of consideration, Elzeth said, "Makes sense. But even if that's true, how do we go about using that to actually find the farm?"

"Callum," Tomas said. "He knows all the traders and trade routes, if he's trying to hire mercenaries out."

Tomas stood and stretched. A few minutes of walking took him to the burned-out husk of the building that used to be Callum's inn. Smoke still rose from the debris as fires burned where no water could reach. One portion of a wall remained, supporting a window frame. Tomas looked through the burnt frame to the blue sky beyond.

Callum sat, cross-legged, in the dirt of the street about twenty feet from the ruins of his inn. His face, hands, and clothes were covered in soot and ash. As Tomas approached, Callum brought a jug, equally filthy, to his lips. He took an enormous swig, grimaced, then followed it with another.

"He might not be too eager to speak to you," Elzeth pointed out.

"Tough. He deserved no less for letting that happen in his inn."

Tomas stopped a couple of paces from Callum and waited for the innkeeper to notice him.

"Whaddya want?" Callum slurred.

"The man who hired you all. The one who burned down your inn."

"Never seen him before." Callum fought a war to get each word out. Tomas figured Callum wasn't on his first jug.

"There's a caravan that makes a stop outside of town. Who guards it?"

Callum took another pull of the jug, then looked disappointed. He held it out in front of him and turned it over. Nothing came out. With one sudden movement, he launched the jug into the ruins of his inn. It shattered.

Callum chuckled grimly. "Only one was ever good enough for them. Only one who could keep her mouth shut." His gaze traveled up to Tomas, and his laughter had an edge of madness to it.

"Her name is Mary, and she was the one who came closest to killing you last night."

24

Callum was more than willing to give up Mary's current location. Once Tomas had it, he was on the move, crossing Razin yet again.

Apparently, after Callum's inn burned down, she'd made it clear she would be staying at the other inn in town. One she had loudly proclaimed as being nicer anyway.

Mary's actions left Tomas feeling uneasy. She'd been smarter than the other mercenaries and had at least guessed what Tomas was. Perhaps there was no love lost between her and Callum, but it still seemed an unusual choice to so publicly insult Callum's inn. After all, he wasn't just an innkeeper, but a connection to work and money. To burn that relationship in the ashes of Callum's misfortune struck Tomas as being both unnecessary and unwise.

She'd lost an ally and made herself easy to find.

Which, perhaps, was the point.

Mary had been clever. Was she setting him another trap?

He supposed the easiest way to find out was to walk into it and see what happened.

"You could ask for help," Elzeth said. "It's not like we're at full strength."

"I'd rather come to Angela with something certain," Tomas said. "I doubt Mary's put together anything worth worrying about. And that's assuming she's even planned a trap. It's possible she's just an ass."

"You just want to impress Angela," Elzeth grumbled.

Tomas didn't dignify the accusation with a response, and Elzeth sighed in resignation.

The other inn was named Razin's Inn, as though Callum's didn't even qualify. Tomas supposed that now, it didn't. The inn was the tallest building on the north-south main street, three stories tall. From his earlier investigation, Tomas knew the inn also ran a large stable behind the building.

A lone swordsman stood watch over the entrance, but he did little more than give Tomas a brief glance. Tomas pushed the door open and stepped into a different world.

Some part of him understood Razin had rivers of money flowing through it. Angela couldn't afford the number of deputies she had if it didn't. But it was still a frontier town, too young to have adopted some of the more expensive tastes that had developed out east. And, Tomas supposed with a grin, Angela had actually tried to keep him away from the nicer parts of town when he'd first arrived.

Thick velvet curtains hung over the windows, keeping the place dim even though the sun still burned bright in the sky. Scents of perfume, wine, and roasted meat mingled in the air. All the servers were women, dressed in frilly dresses that revealed just a hint too much.

Tomas swore under his breath. He'd traveled hundreds of miles, and still the east reached out to him, devouring the simple life usually found at the edge of civilization.

He forced a smile onto his face as one of the servers invited him to sit. He told her he was here to meet someone, and she sauntered away, her hips swaying more than was strictly necessary.

Tomas' eyes took a moment to adjust to the dim room, but as they did, he looked around. Mary wasn't hard to find. She was sitting at the bar, watching him out of the corner of her eye.

Tomas weaved his way around the tables, filled with men and women dressed in the nicest clothing he'd ever seen on this side of the Tershall River. His own attire earned him a few curious looks, but he paid them no mind. He sat down next to Mary, then waved away the bartender as he approached.

"Not thirsty?" Mary asked.

"Too rich for me."

"The drinks are a lot better here than at Callum's."

Tomas ignored the invitation. "You've been delivering supplies directly from a trading caravan to a farm outside Razin."

She was good. He was watching her but didn't see even a flicker of emotion.

"Doesn't seem like something I would do."

"You're going to tell me where you've been delivering those supplies."

"Can't tell you what I don't know."

"What's your price?"

She studied her drink. Looked at him, then back at her drink. She rotated it gently in her hands. "Just how good do you think you are?"

Tomas wasn't sure how to answer that question. She gave him one more look, then came to a decision. "They'll know it was me."

"If they're all dead, not quite sure how it'll matter."

She took a long pull of her drink. "I don't think you understand what you're up against."

"I would if someone would tell me."

She shook her head. "I'll give you the location, nothing more, but first, you need to do something for me."

"What?"

"I owe a merchant here a considerable sum of money. I'd like you to make my debt disappear."

"How am I supposed to do that?"

She raised an eyebrow. "You're the hero of Razin! Everyone's talking about how you saved that boy, then helped Angela defend the town. I'm sure you'll be able to convince a merchant to ignore one past-due bill."

When Tomas didn't immediately agree, she shrugged. "Only way you're going to get my help. What you're asking is risky, and you don't look like the kind of guy who can afford my services."

Tomas supposed he didn't have much choice. He didn't fancy trying to fight the information out of her, especially here. "Fine."

She finished her drink and stood. "Follow me."

Outside, Mary stretched and smiled. "So, where are you from, Tomas?"

He narrowed his eyes at the sudden friendliness, and she shrugged. "No point walking in silence, right?" She led the way through town, and Tomas followed a few steps behind.

"Nowhere in particular," he answered. "Been wandering for a while."

"Why didn't you take Callum up on his offer when he first tried to hire you?"

"Spent a lot of years taking orders. Not keen on returning to the practice."

She nodded at that. "Fair enough. So why stick your neck out for people you don't even know?"

"Why do you work for people who kidnap children?"

"Not my children. And the money's good."

Her answer disappointed him more than it made him angry. It was an honest answer, at least.

Mary turned into an alley between two taller buildings, deep in shadow as the sun fell.

He couldn't say what alarmed him. Nothing in her posture or gait changed. But all at once, every hair on the back of his neck stood straight, like soldiers at attention.

Tomas drew his sword as Mary spun. Elzeth flared, lending Tomas an extra bit of speed. His sword knocked the knife out of Mary's leading hand, but she didn't halt her advance. She kept turning, her trailing hand hidden out of sight. Tomas let the momentum of his swing twist him around. They danced around one another, but Tomas was just fast enough. He drove the pommel of his sword against Mary's forehead, and then she was sprawled on the ground. A knife dropped into the dirt of the alley. Even in shadow, Tomas saw the steel coated in something that was no doubt hazardous to his health. He kicked the poisoned blade away with the toe of his boot.

He hadn't hit her hard enough to knock her unconscious, and Mary seemed a woman of stout constitution. She came to full awareness quickly enough, glaring daggers at him.

"Why try?" Tomas asked. "You knew you'd lose any duel."

"Wasn't planning on dueling," she said, spitting into the dirt. "Figured if someone was willing to pay so much for your corpse last night, they might be willing to part with some of that gold today for the same service."

"You weren't hired?"

She shook her head.

"Where do you deliver the goods on the caravans you escort?"

She spat more blood into the dirt. "Not going to say. Their money's far better than anything you're offering."

Tomas glanced down at the sword he held, wondering if she'd somehow forgotten he literally held her life in his hands.

She grinned at the implied threat. "You're the hero of the town. The kind of guy who sticks his neck into trouble because he thinks it's the right thing to do. So what are you going to threaten me with?"

Tomas remembered Robick's head exploding as the bullet passed through it. The way his emaciated frame dropped to the ground as his life was stolen from him one final time.

He stabbed his sword deep into the meaty part of Mary's thigh.

She cursed and swore at him, but he left the sword buried. "Not that kind of hero."

She stopped struggling and looked up at him. He let her study his face and draw her own conclusions.

She debated for a moment longer, then began to talk.

25

T all stalks of wheat blew gently as the early evening breeze passed over them. Tomas, crouched among the harvest, watched the farmhouse with wary eyes.

There were people inside, though he couldn't tell the exact number. The curtains were drawn, restricting Tomas to counting the passing of silhouettes.

A deputy grunted, and Angela stirred behind him. "Are you sure about this?"

Tomas had his doubts. Mary currently sat in one of Angela's cells, recovering from her wounds. Lying to him wasn't in her best interests, and he trusted she understood that. Still, all he had was Mary's word, which was hard to trust.

At first glance, nothing about the farmhouse seemed extraordinary. It was larger than average, but not so large that it would draw attention. A rambler surrounded by fields of wheat. A small pond reflected Tolkin's moonlight about two hundred feet behind the house. Had Tomas been riding by, he would have passed the house without a second thought.

One more farmhouse in a land increasingly dotted with them.

A prolonged study, though, revealed odd details.

For one, that anyone was up at this time of night. Tomas knew little about farming, but most farmers and settlers he had met were early to bed. Of all their resources, daylight was possibly their most precious, and they were usually up with the rising of the sun. It was several hours past sunset, and the shadows against the curtains hadn't shown any signs of preparing for rest.

The barn also made Tomas uneasy. It was a large structure, bigger than necessary. Not damning in itself, but even in the moonlight Tomas could see the thick chain and enormous padlock securing the doors. Again, by itself, easily explained. Whoever farmed here cared a great deal about protecting the barn.

"No," he admitted, answering Angela's doubts. "It feels like the farm is wrong, somehow, but I was hoping to see something more definitive before we attacked."

"*If* we attack," Angela said. "I don't see anything that justifies me and my deputies breaking onto their property."

"No one said you had to come." One way or the other, Tomas planned on following the lead. If it proved to be nothing, he knew where to find Mary again.

Angela didn't rise to the comment. Tomas hadn't wanted her or the deputies to join him, but had also felt obligated to share what he'd learned when he dragged Mary, bloody and cursing, to the jail.

Any argument between them died when the door to the farmhouse opened. A tall man stepped out, and the light coming from the house silhouetted the sword tied to his hip.

"Enough evidence now?" Tomas asked.

Angela nodded.

The man stood on the porch of the farmhouse, looking out into the dark fields. After a casual study of the landscape, he walked over to the barn and checked on the door. Tomas' sharpened hearing could make out the clanking of the chain as the man tested it. Satisfied, the man returned to the farmhouse. He took one last look around, then went inside.

"I want you two to stay behind," Tomas said as he rose into a crouch.

"Foolish to run in there when you don't know how many stand against you."

"Angela, this is what I did." She knew enough of his history, could guess the types of missions he'd done during the war. "I'll be better in there alone. Easier when you know everyone is an enemy."

She considered for a moment. "Fine. I'll watch the back, in case anyone tries to escape. Gryff can follow you until you get close, then will guard the front entrance."

Tomas looked up at the moon. The night was early yet, and the residents showed no signs of retiring for the evening. No matter. They'd never see him coming. "Twenty minutes or so, then I'll enter."

She nodded, then gave Gryff instructions. She disappeared into the tall wheat.

Tomas waited a few minutes, then gestured for Gryff to follow him. The deputy obeyed, never more than a few paces behind. They crouched and walked, hunched over, through the wheat, nice and slow. Twenty minutes was more than enough time. They made it within fifty feet of the front door, with no sign they'd yet been spotted. For a group that had terrorized the city, they seemed awfully comfortable in their hideout.

Tomas watched the house, able now to hear some of the sounds from the open windows. Sounded like an argument, and a loud one, too. It faded just as Tomas focused on it.

Would have been nice to know the subject of the disagreement. Maybe one of them would share it, later.

He looked for any clue as to what the purpose of the house was. What was so important it would cost so many lives and be worth so much risk?

When he was reasonably certain Angela was in place, he turned to Gryff and whispered that he would go ahead. Gryff nodded as he wiped the sweat from his hands on his shirt. The deputy's eyes were wide, and Tomas heard the man's heart racing.

Tomas took one last look, then ran, Elzeth burning bright. He covered the last feet to the house in several long paces, eyes focused on his destination.

Not the door.

Though he believed he was unnoticed, he wouldn't take any chances with the primary route of entry. It could easily be trapped, guarded, or even barred shut from the inside.

He chose instead a window near the front door. It was open to let in the cool breeze.

Tomas landed one heavy footstep on the porch and then dove.

His leap carried him through the window with no problem. The closed curtains parted as he passed through them, and he had one moment to see he'd jumped into a room with three men inside.

Tomas landed on his shoulder and tumbled. He hit a man with his heels, stopping him halfway through the roll. The man grunted against the impact.

Tomas scrambled to his feet. His eyes darted left and right as his head swiveled. Two men were in the room with him, both bearing the tattoos that identified them as Family.

These men almost certainly knew the sniper that had killed Robick. He drew his sword as the men realized the danger they were in. One cut killed the man he'd rolled into.

The second managed to shout for help before Tomas cut off his plea prematurely. His sword opened the man's throat, swallowing the rest of his cry.

The house erupted with activity. Perhaps they hadn't been ready for an assault, but when one arrived, they responded with admirable haste.

Tomas left the room he'd entered. A sitting room, from the arrangement of the furniture. He strode into the hallway that connected to the front door.

Empty.

Heavy breathing on the other side of the wall, in the dining room. Waiting behind the door frame.

Tomas planted one heavy step, then rolled into the room. An ax split the air above him. Unlike the roll that brought him into the house, this one carried him smoothly to his feet. The man swinging the ax had misjudged his swing. As Tomas stood, the man was fighting against the rotation of the imbalanced weapon. Tomas stabbed his sword through the man's back, piercing a lung.

Loud footsteps pounded behind Tomas. He turned as a young man shouted.

The boy was skilled. His cut was clean, his footwork precise. Two cuts forced Tomas back toward the hallway.

The Family swordsman possessed no obvious faults in his technique, but he was too slow against Tomas and Elzeth. Tomas broke his guard.

He cut through the boy's right bicep, and the arm went limp. A kick to the chest smashed him into a wall. The

Family swordsman slid down the wall slowly, staring at his right arm as though he'd never seen it before.

Tomas let the young man live. He couldn't have been more than eighteen or nineteen.

It wasn't pure mercy, though. Tomas wanted someone alive to answer his questions.

He continued into the kitchen. Two men waited for him. One threw a handful of flour at his face. Thanks to Elzeth, Tomas had enough time to close his eyes and hold his breath. He squatted down against the cut he knew was coming, then used the back of his left hand to wipe the flour from his face.

Tomas opened his eyes in time to see the man who'd thrown the flour step forward, bringing his sword straight down on Tomas' head.

Tomas fell backward, the only action he could take to avoid the killing cut. The man stepped forward into the space Tomas had vacated, leading with his sword.

Behind him, the second Family member cut down at Tomas, too.

Tomas rolled over his hip, barely avoiding the swing. He scrambled again to his feet, but was barely on his feet when the second assailant charged into him. Their swords met between them, and the force of the blow slammed the blunt side of Tomas' sword into his body.

The second Family member was quite a bit larger than Tomas, and he grinned as he pressed his advantage. Tomas gave ground, trying to recover his balance. He ran into something hard and metal.

The sudden burning up and down his hip told him what he'd run into. A hot stove.

The large warrior maintained the pressure on the swords with one hand, then used his other to push Tomas' head toward the stove top. The heat singed the hair on the side of his head.

But he couldn't fight the pressure. The first swordsman was approaching, sword ready. And Tomas had never gotten his feet under him. The only way to fight against the man's strength was to push against the stove, which would burn his hand and render him nearly useless with his sword.

Slowly, inexorably, Tomas' head was pushed closer and closer to the stove.

26

Tomas fought, but without firm footing, he had no leverage against the man. All his strength, and it was mostly useless.

The Family had been cooking something, the stove still burning hot. As the man forced Tomas' head down, the skin around his right eye began to burn. The smell stung his nostrils.

The other enemy, approaching with his sword point first, stabbed at Tomas, and there was nothing for him to do. The man stabbed gently, afraid of hurting his companion, but the tip of his sword still went in and scraped against one of Tomas' ribs. The man drew the blade out, dripping blood, and prepared to stab again.

Tomas roared, but it did nothing to improve his situation. His feet kicked and scrambled for purchase against the floor, but he couldn't get any traction. Nor could he get his body positioned to effectively kick at his assailant.

He swore and let go of his sword with his left hand. Closing his eyes against the pain he knew was coming, he pressed his left palm onto the hot stove.

He'd never imagined it would hurt so much. The pain took a moment to reach his brain, but it exploded with all the force of dynamite in his head. It was a boiling wave of agony, of heat that somehow kept increasing across his hand. The smell of burnt skin hit a moment later, adding insult to injury.

He pushed against the pain, afraid he would soon pass out.

It gave him the leverage he needed.

He shoved with everything he had. It pushed him up and forced the large man back. Tomas' feet found the floor, and he braced his rear boot against the stove. Heaving with his right arm, he sent his tormentor shuffling back several steps.

He couldn't see well out of his right eye, but he didn't dare try to wipe it.

The man who'd stabbed him stepped forward to attack again, but Tomas had his feet. Elzeth and one good arm was all he needed. The man stabbed, but Tomas swiped it away contemptuously. Before the swordsman could recover, Tomas turned his deflection into a cut. The man fell before he even realized he'd been bested.

The larger man swung, but his attack was clumsy. Tomas leaned back and let the sword pass before him. His own cut, even one-handed, was too fast for the brute to respond to.

As the body fell, Tomas listened for others, but the house was silent. He grimaced. No hosts, as far as he could tell.

Or inquisitors.

But this house meant something. No other reason for so many Family to be here.

He refused to look at his left hand. Either they'd been

better than he expected, or he was getting sloppy. This house shouldn't have been this hard to clear.

He continued through the kitchen. There were bedrooms and a washroom, but all were empty. The silence of the house hadn't been a lie.

Tomas found the back door and opened it. He stepped through slowly and shouted into the darkness. "Clear!"

He returned inside. His initial exploration hadn't revealed much. It was a farmhouse, filled with beds and a few functional rooms. It was meant to hold a small army of people. There were more than a dozen beds, bunked four to a room.

It was difficult to think clearly through the pain. His left hand still felt as though he was holding it against the stove. Whenever he moved, he felt the air across his skin as if it were filled with needles.

A memory bloomed in the recesses of his mind. One of the old sword masters at the school that had raised him, lecturing on the philosophy of the sword. Telling the young kids that sometimes it would be necessary to open one's self to injury and death to achieve victory.

He'd swallowed that bitter pill with delight as a child. The words had dripped with glory, which was the only nectar he needed.

Tomas fought the urge to spit on the floor of the house.

The lesson wasn't false. Not exactly.

But the advice hadn't been pure. Now, Tomas knew the sword schools were funded by the army. They collected the outcasts and the orphans, and when the students graduated, they had positions waiting for them in the service. For the cost of some meager food, a leaky roof, and instruction from retired sword masters, the army inherited hundreds of nearly perfect soldiers per year.

It was a complicated thing. Tomas retained some vague memories of the streets, and knew that he was grateful for his time in the school. It had been tough, but they'd given him skills he never could have acquired elsewhere. And he'd always had food and shelter, meager as it was.

Still, knowing what he knew now, it felt like something had been stolen from him.

Tomas forced himself to look at his hand. The burns made his stomach queasy.

The tough old bastard would have approved, though.

Tomas reached the entryway of the house. The front door was standing open. He frowned.

The door had been closed earlier. He had come in through the window. Gryff? But there was no one else in the house. Tomas heard nothing.

He went to the door and looked out. The night was quiet. "Gryff!"

There was no answer. Tomas' stomach sank. He took cover behind the door frame.

He waited for a few moments, watching for any signs of movement in the grass. But the house was lit by lanterns, and he couldn't see well, even with Elzeth's aid. Tomas broke from the cover of the house and sprinted across the grass, half-expecting the host's rifle to echo across the plains.

He reached the tall grass without problem and took cover. The blades of grass felt like dragging razors across his burned left hand. He kept low, working his way toward the place where he'd left Angela's deputy.

Tomas smelled Gryff before he saw him. In his last moments, he'd lost control of his bowels.

Tomas swore when he saw the body. A knife had been driven through the man's eye.

The deputy had never even gotten a shot off with his rifle.

27

Tomas' examination of Gryff's body didn't take long. The cause of death was obvious enough, and the nature of the scene only allowed for one suspect. Unless Gryff was the one untrained deputy on Angela's pay, a host was responsible.

He kept low to the ground and sprinted across the open space in front of the house, but no gunshots followed him. Tomas still wasn't convinced the host had run too far, but it seemed that they weren't waiting in ambush. He let Angela know he was in the house and heard her answering call from several rooms away.

She was tearing through one of the bedrooms, but stopped when she saw his disfigurement. "Are you okay? What happened?"

"Got too close to a stove."

"How bad is it?"

"Pretty bad, but I'll heal."

She accepted his claim and turned back to the bedroom. "Where's Gryff?"

"He's dead."

Her head snapped around.

"I think the host was here when I entered. They left through the front door when I was fighting in the kitchen. They killed Gryff without him even getting a shot off."

Angela swore and made for the front door, but Tomas held out his hand. "I'm not sure it's safe outside yet. Let's finish examining the place, and then we can take care of him together."

Her nostrils flared, but she took several long breaths and nodded.

She performed her investigation while Tomas watched. Occasionally, he'd return to the front door and look outside, but he never saw any movement in the grasses beyond.

Angela's search was thorough. Every piece of clothing was examined, every drawer and cupboard throughout the house was opened. She confiscated a box of ammo, worth more than most farmers made in a year. But otherwise, her detailed search revealed nothing Tomas' quick glance had missed.

With every room, Tomas saw the tension building within the marshal. He kept his lips sealed, guessing her desire.

When her search finished in the living room, she punched the wall hard enough to leave a hole. "What are they doing?"

She didn't turn to look at him, and he didn't answer. He had none to give.

She pulled her fist from the wall and turned sharp on her heel. Her eyes were red-rimmed, but her voice was just as cold as his wounds burned. "Let's see Gryff."

He nodded and led the way, expecting a protest that never came. She followed close behind as he ran across the open space, then crouched as he did. He led her to her deputy, then turned to give her some room.

She grabbed his good wrist and held it. "Stay." Her voice came out as a hoarse whisper. "Please."

He acquiesced, and together they knelt next to Gryff.

Her grief was silent, but it shook her body. She gripped his good hand tightly. In time, she looked up to the sky, and Tomas saw the trails tears had left down her cheek.

"He was the only one of us with a family," she said. "Wife and two boys. He was so excited to raise them out here, away from the city."

Tomas squeezed her hand a little tighter.

"Haven't lost a soldier since the war. Promised myself that I never would again. It's one of the reasons I run this town like I do. Less trouble you allow, the less chance something like this happens."

"We'll find them," Tomas said.

She shook her head. "I just want them gone." She took a deep, shuddering breath. "When I came here, I hoped that I would be putting the war behind me. But it keeps reaching out, wanting to draw me back in until I'm no better than the mercenaries who spend their nights retelling stories at Callum's place."

"Or wandering the west?" Tomas added, finishing her unspoken accusation.

She nodded.

"You've made this a place to be proud of," Tomas said. "I'll help you protect it."

"How? We've got no more leads."

"This isn't over. Now, we've stirred the hornet's nest. Tonight, you return to Razin and collect the rest of your deputies. You'll bring them back and search the barn. Whatever is in there is important. The Family were guarding it."

"What about you?"

Tomas grimaced. He didn't like sending Angela out alone, not knowing where the host had run off to, but there wasn't much choice. He feared if they left the house unguarded, they'd return to find it burned to the ground, or any evidence otherwise gone. "I'll stay here and keep watch over Gryff. You can bring a cart when you bring the others. I'll make sure nothing happens to him or the house."

He could see she debated the wisdom of his advice, but she didn't have any better plans. "I'll be back soon."

With that she was gone, disappearing in the grass in the direction of their horses.

She hadn't been gone for more than a moment when Elzeth spoke. "You want me to work on your injuries?"

"How tired are you?"

"Exhausted."

Tomas weighed the possibilities. He wasn't terribly useful without both hands, and the constant pain prevented him from focusing. But if he encountered the host again, he'd need Elzeth.

"You can work on my injuries. I don't suppose you'd be able to keep watch, too?"

"Well enough, I suppose."

"Thanks."

Tomas moved away from Gryff, wanting to at least get himself upwind of the smell. He lay down and stared up at the night sky, the stars twinkling down at him. He noticed his senses dull as Elzeth began the enormous task of healing him once again.

Tired as he was, he expected to fall asleep immediately.

Maybe a half hour later, Elzeth made fun of him. "Hard to sleep?"

"Guess so."

"Her?"

Tomas nodded. "She's found a new way. First time I've probably said this about anyone, but she deserves to be marshal."

"Jealous?"

"Yeah."

Elzeth didn't reply for some time. "Ever think that maybe this is your way? What you've been doing for all these years? You've been wandering for a long time like this."

"Thought's occurred to me. Don't like it much, though. I want to settle down, but it doesn't ever feel right when I find a place, even one like this."

Elzeth chuckled. "The assassination attempts aren't very welcoming."

Tomas laughed softly at that, then grimaced as the pain in his chest flared. "That they are not."

Tomas considered the trail of destruction that had followed his arrival. He knew he wasn't the cause of it, but all the same, he felt responsible. He thought of Gryff and Angela, and the dream of the future they shared. He clenched his right fist. "When we find them," Tomas said, "I'm going to kill them all."

"I know," Elzeth replied. "I'll be right here, helping."

28

When Elzeth woke Tomas, Shen was nearing the horizon, surrendering the sky to the incoming sun. The faint sound of a cart off in the distance told him Angela and the others were approaching.

"Nothing?" he asked.

"Perfectly quiet," Elzeth answered.

Tomas grunted. He would have bet a fair amount of his remaining coin either the Family or the church would have launched an attack to reclaim the house.

He looked down at his left hand. It still looked burned, but he could open and close it with only minimal pain. "How am I?"

"Your hand should be good enough to fight with, if it comes to that. I've healed the area around your right eye, too, and closed the stab wound on your chest. It'll reopen if you fight, but it's not fatal. I haven't gotten around to healing the burned skin, though."

"You didn't prioritize my good looks?"

"Impossible to save what you never had."

Tomas smiled. The expression pulled and pushed against the burned skin on his face. It hurt, but at a level he could bear.

He pushed himself to his feet to greet the others. Angela had brought not just a deputy, but several other warriors from Razin. The fighters who'd been hired to attack him back at Callum's inn. They visibly stiffened when they saw him.

Angela was on the back of her horse, and she rode ahead of the cart to meet him.

"Hired help?" he asked.

"Not my first choice," she admitted, "but I needed more swords."

Tomas couldn't fault her for that. As a temporary measure, they would suffice.

He climbed onto the cart as it rumbled past. Not even one of the mercenaries met his eye.

They rode down to the farmhouse. Angela ordered the mercenaries to set a perimeter while they worked. The deputy was put in charge of the mercenaries. Angela and Tomas approached the barn, and she produced a key out of her pocket. At Tomas' questioning look, she said, "Found it on the body of one of the Family in the house."

The key fit in the padlock, and the mechanism opened smoothly. Angela pulled the chain free, and together, they opened the massive doors.

The scents of worked leather and oil greeted the two as they stepped inside. Angela carried a lantern, casting the light slowly back and forth.

Tomas had hoped for answers, but a single glance told him that all he could expect were more mysteries. This was no working barn, but instead a building intended solely for storage. Crates and barrels stood piled high in neat rows. They were all labeled with symbols that looked like a code.

Tomas found a crowbar and began working on a few of the crates that were easy to reach. One was filled with bags of flour. Another with rice. Deeper in, one of the crates held sheets of metal, hammered thin and found in a dizzying variety of shapes and forms that he could make no sense of.

Angela called a few of the mercenaries in to lend a hand. She supervised while they opened crate after crate.

Tomas kept half an eye on the proceedings while exploring the barn more thoroughly. Most of what the mercenaries uncovered was more of the same. Plenty of food and supplies, as well as metal, tools, and leather for a project he couldn't begin to imagine. In one small crate, one of the mercenaries found several sealed flasks of different colored liquids.

Tomas had no idea what they were, but he had seen enough to know what this place was.

A supply depot.

Guarded by the Family, for a purpose Tomas couldn't begin to guess at.

But where did the supplies go? They were stored here, brought directly by caravan. It had to be close.

Tomas borrowed a lantern and examined the barn from floor to ceiling. He shuffled crates around, looking for tunnels. By the time he was done he no longer needed the lantern, the sun shining through the wide-open door.

He'd found nothing.

The others were still searching through the crates, Angela supervising, ensuring no detail was missed.

Tomas returned to the house and repeated the search one more time. He created a mental map of the house, checking it against the structure on the outside, making sure no space was unaccounted for. He tapped along the floor, looking for secret passages. His search revealed a root cellar underneath a corner of the kitchen, but the cellar was nothing more than it seemed.

He left the house again and looked around. There were secrets here, but the land held tight to them.

He blinked and yawned. Elzeth was completely still, as tired as he was.

Eventually, they wrapped up their search. Angela stationed the mercenaries and her deputy at the house. They wrapped up Gryff's body and placed it in a coffin in the middle of the cart.

Angela let one of the mercenaries ride her horse back to town beside them. She and Tomas took the cart, and it rumbled slowly back toward town.

Angela noticed Tomas' exhaustion. "You can rest at my place."

He nodded. "None for you?"

"Not yet. I need to talk to Gryff's family, and make sure the town doesn't fall apart."

Tomas nodded again. He was too tired to make much conversation.

When Razin came into view, Tomas felt his stomach sink. From a distance, the town looked peaceful. He saw it as he imagined Angela did. And it was a good place, being eaten from within by a cancer he couldn't find.

"I need to know," Angela said, her thoughts echoing Tomas' own.

He squeezed her hand.

They rode into town, and Angela dropped him off outside her place. She handed him a key.

He looked up at her. The sun was behind her, silhouetting her and casting a halo around her head. He squinted against the light. "You sure you're going to be fine?"

"Get some rest, Tomas." She snapped the reins and the cart creaked forward. Tomas watched as she escorted the coffin on the next part of its journey.

He understood.

This next part, she needed to do alone.

29

After sleeping most of the day and taking a quick bath, Tomas felt nearly human again. Angela had a mirror in her house, which allowed him to check on the progress of his healing. While he'd slept, Elzeth had healed his face and continued work on the wound on his chest. Except for his hand, Tomas' appearance had returned largely to normal. But the hand was functional, which was all Tomas cared about for the moment.

As he dressed, he considered what to do next.

Angela hadn't returned, and Tomas suspected it would be night before she did. There was no obvious next step. After debating a few outlandish ideas, Tomas decided his best choice was to simply wait. Even if they hadn't found the answers they sought, he and Angela had made a ruckus. There would be a response, sooner rather than later.

That mystery wasn't the only reason he'd come to Razin, though.

He left Angela's place, locking the door behind him and pocketing the key. A short walk brought him to the now familiar sights of Ben's place. The gate was shut, but the sounds of children playing could be heard from almost a block away.

Tomas knocked on the gate, and Olena led him in. She was outside, the only adult supervising the children. She gave him a smile and gestured toward the house. "He's been inside all day, looking through his old notebooks."

"Do you mind?" Tomas asked.

"Not at all. Go on in. Someone needs to stay out here to prevent total anarchy."

Tomas weaved his way through running children, narrowly avoiding several flying balls that passed suspiciously close to his head. He waved at Clara, playing with a small group of girls. Then another ball almost hit him.

By the time he got inside, he felt as though he'd strode across a battlefield.

He took off his boots and wandered through the house, passing rooms filled with bunk beds and more toys than he'd ever seen in his life. Eventually, though, he came to a small room near the back of the house, lit by one large window. Ben was within, surrounded by papers. He looked up when Tomas entered. "Figured you might show up today. Were you able to track down the people responsible for the disappearances?"

Tomas caught Ben up, and the former inquisitor didn't let a single detail slip by unexamined. "It's no surprise, I guess," he said, leaning back in his chair with a sigh. "The church has always had layers, deeper than anyone ever expects. Even as an inquisitor, much of the church's purpose was hidden from me."

"You think they're nearby, too?"

Ben nodded. "You hurt them, though. Hiring that many Family, including a host, must have cost a small fortune. They'll have to act."

"Any ideas where to look until then?"

"I'm afraid not."

Tomas put the question away for the moment. More thinking rarely solved any of his problems. "Then what about me?"

"Now that is another interesting problem." Ben flipped through his papers. "Obviously, all my information is far out of date now, but even back when we met, you were one of the longest-lived hosts we'd ever come across. And certainly one of the most sane. You were considered quite an acquisition, you know."

Tomas raised an eyebrow. "Honored."

Ben brushed aside his sarcasm. "The point is, even years ago you were something of an anomaly. None of the documented hosts infected around the same time as you were remotely similar in terms of sanity."

Tomas grunted at the sudden storm in his stomach, and Ben looked up from his papers. "Elzeth doesn't consider himself an infection."

Ben nodded. "Sorry. Old terminology dies hard, I guess. But barring another unique case, your longevity is even more unusual than you think. Our studies found that most hosts lived an average of three and a half years after unity." He glanced at Tomas' stomach, as though hoping for Elzeth's approval of the term.

"That's good and all, but what does it mean?"

"It means that something about one of you, or your bond, is unprecedented. I'll admit, though I've left the inquisition behind, the fact you can sit here and have a conversation burns me with a curiosity I haven't felt in many, many years."

"Am I in danger?"

"You're a wandering swordsman who, I can't help but

notice, seems to find trouble wherever you walk. I'd say you're in danger, yes."

"You know what I mean."

"And you know there's no way for me to answer that question honestly. I've looked through everything. There's no one else like you. There weren't even rumors of another person lasting so long. If there's another like you, the level of church I was on had no idea."

Tomas sighed. After everything, to hit another wall was almost more than he could stand. "So, you have no ideas?"

Ben laughed. "Oh, I have more theories than you would stand to listen to. It could be either you or Elzeth is special in some way. Or perhaps your refusal to use Elzeth unless he's needed has helped you build a resistance to madness. It could just be that you've used your strength sparingly enough that both of you have adapted. You've become a new evolution of host. Stronger and faster than anyone else."

"But you don't know."

"It's all a guess."

Tomas leaned back, mirroring Ben's posture. He crossed his arms, so that he could better fight the urge to punch something.

"May I offer a suggestion, not as a former inquisitor, but simply as an old man?"

"You're not that old."

"No, but I have aged. And you haven't. You look the same as you did back when I tortured you."

"What?"

Ben waved it away. "No matter. What I want to say is this. You came here because you were worried about what your strength might mean for you. What this lack of madness might mean. True?"

Tomas nodded.

"It means nothing."

Tomas unfolded his arms and leaned forward. Ben didn't flinch from his stare, though.

"You're a rational man, Tomas. At least, as rational as any other. Your observations about yourself aren't deluded. You have no tics, and more strength than you used to have. All this is true. So why not simply accept it? It has no meaning beyond the fact that you know you are capable of more than you thought possible."

"But will I go mad?"

"Does it matter?"

"Huh?" Tomas struggled to follow.

"Madness, for you, is little different than death is for any of the rest of us. Perhaps there is some chance you can hold it off forever, that you can avoid the fate that plagues your kind. To me, it seems unlikely. Madness strikes all hosts. You've just figured out a way to hold it back, longer than anyone else. But it strikes me that it doesn't change anything for you. Just as all humans must live with the specter of death riding in the saddle beside us, so must you make peace with your inevitable madness."

Tomas leaned back again in his chair, chewing over Ben's thoughts. Ben gave him a moment, then continued.

"The only meaning your strength has is the meaning you make. Might you allow me to make one further suggestion, this time as the former inquisitor you freed?"

Tomas nodded, still unable to speak.

"Let it all go."

Tomas blinked, then frowned.

"Our pasts shape us. Of that, there is no argument. Though I have left the tools of torture behind, I will always have a mind trained to notice details, prepared to peel away the lies others tell. You know, better than anyone alive, the horrors I've committed. I don't believe I'll ever understand true peace, but I've at least enjoyed a measure of it here. I believe you could do the same, if you ever let the past die."

Tomas considered. He'd heard the same before, most often from other soldiers immediately after the war.

Coming from Ben, though, it had a weight he hadn't felt before.

They sat quietly, the sounds of the children shouting in the yard outside their only company.

"I'm sorry," Ben eventually said, "that I have no better answers for you. You know my guesses, but I'm sure it's nothing you've not already considered. But perhaps I can give you something."

Tomas grunted.

"Come here tomorrow for supper. Olena and I will find someone to watch the children for an hour or two. Let me show you, firsthand, the peace you might find."

At that moment, all Tomas wanted to do was escape from the small room. The walls of notebooks were closing in, threatening to squeeze him alive. He nodded, offered a short bow, and fled. His heart was beating fast, and his palms were sweaty, as though he'd just escaped an ambush.

It wasn't until he was through the yard and out the front gate that he felt like he could breathe again.

He wandered the quiet streets until the sun set. Angela had made no pronouncement Tomas was aware of, but most residents remained inside their homes, hoping to weather out the coming storm in peace.

Tomas felt the storm, both literally and figuratively. The air grew thicker, filled with moisture. The breeze that sometimes seemed a constant companion had faded, leaving the air still and sticky. Fortunately, the sun was setting, keeping

Razin relatively cool. Tomas looked to the sky. Not a cloud to be seen, not even on the horizon.

Which would hit first? The thunderstorm, or the attack he was certain was coming?

He ended his wanderings in front of Angela's home. The key opened the door, and as soon as he stepped in, he knew she was home and asleep. He closed the door quietly behind him, slipped off his boots, and tiptoed through the house.

He found her in her bedroom. She'd left the door open, which he took as an invitation.

He stopped at the door. Angela's breathing was deep and even, and every so often, a soft snore could be heard. He smiled. She was even more beautiful at rest. Her face lost the tension it carried throughout the day.

He couldn't bring himself to walk any farther. She needed the sleep, and he had no wish to disturb her.

Was this what Ben wanted for him? A home to come to, a woman by his side?

He acknowledged the appeal. A life like this would feel safe and stable. Razin was fine, he supposed, so long as it wasn't trying to kill him. He cared for Angela, as much as he'd cared about anyone else in years.

And yet...

He shook his head and sighed silently.

He turned and retreated to the living room, where a couch would make a good enough bed for the evening. Hells, he'd slept in many worse places. He settled in and found a comfortable position.

"I'm a bit of a mess, aren't I?" he said.

Elzeth stirred. "Nothing I haven't been saying for years."

Tomas stared up at the ceiling, exhausted but unable to sleep.

"You think he's right?"

"I think he's got a point about not worrying about tics or madness. We made a decision long ago not to use our strength any more than necessary. Seems to me, nothing's really changed. Just because it seems like we can do more, doesn't mean we should."

Tomas acknowledged the point.

"But I don't think you should accept Ben's answer as your own."

"No?"

"You're happiest when you're out, exploring new places. A domestic existence doesn't suit you."

Tomas felt himself relax. "Thanks, partner."

"Any time. Now get to sleep so I can finish healing you."

Tomas' sleep that night was restorative. At least until morning came, bringing with it the next attack.

30

Tomas woke to the sound of someone pounding on Angela's door. "Marshal!"

Tomas squinted. The sun was barely up.

Angela was at the door in the time it took Tomas to swing his feet off the couch. Remembering her desire to keep his presence quiet, he kept himself out of sight as she opened the door. The voice was familiar. One of her last remaining deputies.

He could overhear the conversation without Elzeth's help.

"The jail was attacked last night," the deputy said. "It was a bloodbath. And on my way over here, I heard that there are other bodies."

"How many?"

"I don't know, but I'm guessing quite a few. The town's about ready to explode."

Angela was silent for a moment. "Go around town. Horseback, if it makes it faster. Talk to people. Find out who's been attacked. Have families check on their neighbors. I want a list of everyone who died." She paused. "Why was there no alarm raised?"

The deputy's response was sheepish. "Whoever did it did it real quiet. I was on patrol all night and never heard so much as a cry."

Tomas' ears perked up at that. That was some skill.

"Fine," Angela said. "Get me the list of the dead. Reassure people, if you can."

"How?" The deputy sounded lost.

"Be present. Be visible. Don't let them see you're scared. For most, that will be enough."

"What are you going to do?"

"I'll start at the jail. Then I'll join you and we can finish up around the town together."

There was a rustle of clothes, and then the door was shut. Angela came into the living room. "You heard?"

Tomas nodded. "I'll slip out the back and meet you at the jail."

He did, and a few minutes later he was out on the streets. They were packed with people, clustered tight into small groups. Several citizens nodded at him, but others squirmed a little closer together when he neared. He was still a stranger in this town.

Again, Tomas didn't envy Angela her work. He was coming to believe that war was easier to wage than peace was to maintain.

The door to the jail was open, so Tomas went right in, and stopped just past the threshold. A few moments later, a gasp behind him let him know Angela had arrived.

Blood coated the floor, filling the cracks in the wood. Most of it had dried, except in a few places where it had pooled in depressions. A man was slumped at the front desk, the artery on his neck exposed. Tomas recognized him as a mercenary from Callum's inn.

Angela explained before he could ask. "Needed more fighters. Figured if I paid them enough, they'd be loyal for at least a few days."

Tomas took in the scene at the desk. The mercenary didn't have a single defensive wound. "It happened so fast he didn't even fight."

"The host?"

"Maybe," Tomas said. Something about the wound bothered him.

The scene only grew worse the deeper in they went. The cells were all shut, and every prisoner who'd been within was dead. Mary had died with everyone else.

Tomas clenched his fists. The wounds here weren't clean. Several of the corpses had multiple cuts.

His eyes traveled to the floor. Blood was everywhere here, too, but there was only one set of boot prints. There were no other marks.

In a flash of insight, he knew why the wounds bothered him. The mercenary had been on the other side of a desk. These victims were on the other side of steel bars. He knew who had done this.

Angela must have seen the expression on his face change. "What?"

"This was the inquisitor."

"How do you know?"

Tomas pointed down to the floor. "None of the cell doors were opened. And several of the corpses are backed up into the corner, all with stab wounds. That's the same weapon Ben uses. The same weapon many inquisitors are trained in. Whip it in through the bars and keep stabbing until the prisoner dies."

Angela turned pale. "They were trapped with no way to defend themselves."

Tomas nodded. "And the walls are thick enough they could have screamed for help all night and no one would have heard." He let himself imagine the scene, just for a moment.

He clenched his fists.

The church was already stained with sin, but they were always eager to find new ways to cover themselves in filth.

Tomas went to the end of the hall, where he said the old words next to the last jail cell. Then he went to the next and repeated the process. Angela watched him, then said, "I'm going out to learn the extent of the damage. Find me when you can."

She left him then, to mourn those who had lost their lives the night before.

Saying the words over them all brought some small comfort to his heart. But he wouldn't be satisfied. Not until he'd brought the church to justice.

He didn't have much time. He suspected the church's motive.

The sun nearly blinded him when he stepped out of the jail. If it was possible, the streets were even more crowded than before. Commerce and daily activity had ground to a halt. People remained huddled together in clumps. He asked after Angela and was told she'd run in the direction of Razin's Inn.

Tomas had to give her credit. He guessed she'd also figured out the church's motives. He followed her, arriving at the building just as she was leaving. From the color of her face, he guessed the scene hadn't been much different from the jail.

"All mercenaries?" he asked.

She nodded. "You guessed?"

"They're killing all the witnesses. Cleaning up their tracks. They'll be leaving soon."

She nodded again. "Looks like the same type of weapon. They were all killed in their sleep. No one saw anything. Callum is dead, too." She recited the facts as though she was giving a report. She was still dazed.

"Are there any other bodies?"

"A few. Looks like most were here and in the jail. One was staying with family here in town. There's a citizen dead, too. Not sure why, but I'm guessing if I look hard enough, I'll find some sort of connection."

"Any evidence we can use?"

She shook her head. "It's like we were attacked by a ghost. No one saw anything. I've got the murderer's boot print, but what good is that? I'm certain it isn't anyone in town."

Tomas thought for a moment. "I can go back to the farmhouse. Maybe in the light of day I'll find something."

It was a poor idea, and they both knew it. They'd searched the farmhouse thoroughly before they left. But it was the only lead he could think of. It served another purpose, too.

"You'll see if they're alive?" Angela asked.

"I will," Tomas said.

"Bring them back if they are," she said. "There's nothing there that's worth more lives."

31

When the farmhouse came into view, Tomas breathed a sigh of relief. One of the mercenaries Angela had hired was slowly circling the grounds. The house and barn stood, just as they'd left them. The mercenary saw him and waved.

He was grateful to find that nothing was amiss, but at the same time, frustrated.

The supplies they'd captured were worth a small fortune. Some, such as the chemicals, had to be hard to acquire, transport, and store, making them even more valuable. If the church was preparing to flee, he expected them to attack the farmhouse.

His shadowy foe didn't act as he expected, which left him reactive, unable to gain an advantage.

He rode into the front yard and dismounted. As soon as he stood still, he began to sweat, the humidity and sun assaulting him together. The day was shaping up to be a scorcher. He wiped the sleeve of his shirt across his forehead.

"Hot enough for you?" the mercenary asked.

"And then some," Tomas answered.

"When it breaks, it's going to be a storm to remember."

Tomas nodded, and just then, the deputy came out. He looked bored. It only took a few minutes for both sides to catch up. The farmhouse had been quiet. No one had seen or heard anything last night.

They were surprised to hear about the chaos back in Razin. But when Tomas told the mercenaries they should collect their pay and get out of town, no one argued. While the others prepared to leave, Tomas made one last search of the grounds, but there was nothing. He remained while the others left, scouring the place for clues.

He was no more successful than he had been before.

Tomas swore as he wiped more sweat from his brow. His shirt was getting so soaked it wasn't even working as a towel anymore.

He looked around.

"I hate this," Tomas said.

Elzeth, who'd been quiet all day, said nothing. Tomas felt the sagani's frustration as acutely as his own.

With nothing else to do, he mounted the horse Angela had loaned him and rode back to Razin.

The town, to his surprise, soldiered on despite the murders and the overwhelming heat of the day. Customers visited shops. Carts rumbled down streets, filled with goods. The market square was particularly busy, as merchants set up canvas coverings over their stalls. When Tomas inquired, he learned that a caravan was expected in the next day or two.

He found Angela not far from the square. She was speaking with two men when he arrived, and he waited for her to finish.

The men departed, their concerns addressed, and Angela gave him a tired smile. "Anything?"

"Nothing. How are you?"

"Tired. Frustrated. Hot."

"Any way I can help?"

She shrugged. "Not much to do. They've left us nothing. Anyone who might have said anything is dead, or too scared to talk." She looked up and down the streets. "You can keep watch, if you want, but I don't think they'll attack again."

"You don't think so?"

She shook her head. "Who's left to kill? The mercenaries that were at the farmhouse are leaving town with their tails between their legs, and truth be told, I don't much care what happens to them."

"What about Ben?"

"If they didn't attack him yesterday, I doubt they will today. He'll be on guard now. No, I expect that they've done all they intend to. They're on the run."

Tomas hoped she was wrong. Her theory would bring peace to Razin, which he knew was all she wanted. But he couldn't stand the idea of the church getting away with all they'd done. He wanted them close, where he and Elzeth could reach them.

But he couldn't say any of that.

"Ben invited me for dinner tonight."

"Going?"

Tomas nodded.

Angela gave him a sly smile. "Well, I guess I'll just have to wait up tonight."

The invitation made Tomas smile, too. "I guess you will."

He left Angela to her work. With a little time to spare, he returned to her place for a quick nap. He woke, feeling more refreshed than he had in days.

At Ben's he was greeted by Clara. She studied him with those wide eyes that seemed to see more than they should. "I heard Mister Ben and Miz Olena talking about you," she proclaimed. "They said you're a host. Is it true?"

Tomas nodded.

"You don't look any different than anyone else to me," she decided.

"Did you expect me to?"

"Kind of."

"Sorry to disappoint you."

"That's okay. You seem nice enough. Are you here for our tea party?"

Tomas admired the girl's acceptance of who he was. It almost hurt him to admit he wasn't here for her. "Not today, but soon."

It appeared Ben had hired one of the young women of Razin to watch the children for the evening, and she finally called for Clara to join them. The girl ran away, waving at Tomas as she left.

Tomas watched her go, then knocked at the door to the house. Ben opened the door, releasing the smell of roasted garlic and onion. Tomas' mouth immediately watered. He took off his boots and came in. Olena greeted him warmly, then turned her attention back to the kitchen.

Ben and Tomas walked to Ben's study, where they talked about the past day in quiet tones. They'd barely finished when Olena called them to the table.

They sat at one end of the long table, with Ben at the head and Olena and Tomas sitting across from one another. It felt odd to be eating at a table with so much empty space, but it made their small gathering somehow feel even more intimate.

They ate slowly. Tomas tried to limit the conversation to

polite topics, and Ben seemed eager to do the same. But by the time they'd finished their main course, Olena looked like she was about to explode. She cleared their plates, and when she returned, carried three mugs of ale. She slammed them down on the table. "I thought perhaps you two needed a little help remembering how to be interesting."

Tomas was shocked, but Ben grinned. "What would you like to hear, dear?"

"I want Tomas to tell me how you two escaped the church."

"I've told you that story at least a dozen times!" Ben protested.

"And I've never heard it once from Tomas," Olena calmly answered.

They both turned to him, and Tomas belatedly realized his jaw was hanging open.

Ben chuckled.

"She...knows?" Tomas asked.

"She's my wife," Ben said. "Did you think I'd keep that much of my past from her?"

Tomas stuttered for a bit, then clenched his jaw shut. He took a breath and then a big swallow of ale. "I suppose I did, yes."

And so, Tomas found himself retelling the story, from his capture to his escape. At times, Olena interrupted with questions, each one detailed enough for Tomas to realize Ben had held nothing back from her.

When he finished the story, he looked at the couple with new eyes. Finding a wife with a heart as big as Olena's was no small feat for any man. But for Ben to succeed, and for her to know his past, left him speechless. "When did you learn?" he blurted.

"The day he asked for my hand in marriage," Olena said.

"He proposed but told me there was something I had to know first."

"And you still said 'yes'?"

"I knew him well enough." She answered without hesitation.

"How?" Tomas realized his questions were rude, but his curiosity overwhelmed his sense of decorum.

"We were spending every day together," Olena said. "I saw the generosity in his heart, and though he tried to hide it, I also saw the demons he fought against. It was that, really, that made me love him. I saw him trying so hard to be a better man."

Ben jumped in. "I knew she was observant. I think some part of me always respected that about her. But I thought I hid my struggles well."

Olena put her hand over Ben's and squeezed it. "I remember one day, when we were walking down a street. It was in the city, mind you, so not like here. A drunk man came up to us and was very rude. He started pushing at Ben. Then, the lecherous jerk made a grab for me." She took a sip of ale. "Ben had been patient enough, but when the man reached for me, Ben moved so fast I hardly saw it. The whole incident only lasted a few seconds. But in that moment, I saw the fire in Ben's heart, and I also watched him master it. The way Ben moved, I just knew he could have hurt that man. Or killed him. But Ben simply pushed him away, and we went on with our date."

Tomas leaned back in his chair, watching the two of them. Olena's thumb brushed the back of Ben's hand, rubbing it gently.

Tomas felt something loosen in his chest. He pushed his chair back and stood up. "Thanks for having me." He bowed toward the couple. "Truly."

Ben stood as well, resting his hand for a moment on Olena's shoulder. Together, the two men walked to the front door. Ben escorted him through the tornado of playing children and to the front gate. He stopped Tomas before he could leave. "Thanks for coming," he said. "Do you understand, now, what you gave me?"

Tomas nodded. "You're a lucky man."

"True, but it's not just luck. The same future is open to you, if you allow it."

"Someday, perhaps," was as much as Tomas would grant.

Ben didn't push the matter, though Tomas thought he might. Instead, he changed the subject and cautioned Tomas further. "I fear you're wrong about the church," he said.

"How so?"

"You're right to guess they are killing all the connections to whatever they're doing, but it's not because they're planning on leaving."

Tomas frowned.

"You're thinking more like a military commander than a believer. You assume that because you've dealt them a crippling blow, they'll retreat. It's rational, and what you would do if your positions were reversed. But the church doesn't retreat, because it never believes it can be beaten."

"So why the killings?"

Ben shrugged. "Couldn't say for sure. I suspect they're eliminating anyone who knew anything. Anyone who saw or experienced something they shouldn't have. They're buying themselves a fresh start with the blood of others." He sighed. "You're more than capable of watching after yourself, but don't let your guard down. The threat hasn't passed. If anything, it's greater than ever. I know I won't be sleeping tonight."

32

Tomas left Ben's place feeling a strange mixture of emotions. He was genuinely happy for the former inquisitor, pleased to see that something good could come from a horrible past. It was like watching a flower emerge from a dung heap.

If Ben could find it, there was no reason he couldn't, too.

Like Ben, there was more blood in his past than he cared to think about. Sins that couldn't and shouldn't be forgiven.

He wandered the streets of Razin for a bit, but the sun was setting, and he knew that no matter how long he walked, he'd find no new answers. He'd been walking for years, and he was as confused today as he was when he'd helped Ben escape from the clutches of the inquisitors. Eventually, he turned and made his way to Angela's house.

She was there, in the dining room, finishing up her own supper.

He sat down, passing on her offer of some of her meal. He'd eaten well with Ben and Olena.

"You look like you've just come from a funeral," she said.

He forced a smile onto his face. "Not nearly. If anything,

it was one of the nicest meals I've had in some time. I'm very happy for Ben and what he's done."

"I hear a big 'but' in there," she said.

"But it makes me ask a lot of questions. Makes me doubt a lot of beliefs I've held for years."

"Such as?"

"For a long time, I kept moving farther west," he said. "I've been all the way to the edges of settled land and pushed even further. I believed the only way I'd find any measure of peace was to build a house out in the middle of nowhere."

"Razin's not that close to the middle of nowhere," Angela pointed out. "In a few years, it's going to be pretty much the center of this whole area."

"I know. I got caught up in a few events, ended up having to backtrack all the way to the railroad. And now I'm here, and it's not what I expected."

He saw the question in her eyes, but she didn't ask it. He met her gaze. "Despite the number of people trying to kill me, I like Razin. You're one of the first marshals I've come across worthy of the badge you wear. It's the first time I've been someplace and really thought I could settle here."

"What does Elzeth think?" Angela asked.

It was the first time she'd spoken the sagani's name, and it sent a thrill through them both. Angela only knew it because Ben had spoken it aloud, and Ben was perhaps the only person alive who'd ever heard the name uttered.

"He's got mixed feelings. Both of us have more questions about being a host than answers, and part of our wandering has been in service to seeking out those answers. But we've been walking for a long time, and we're not much closer to understanding what we are than we were before. Ben actually told us to stop worrying about it so much, to simply accept that we are what we are."

"Can you?"

Tomas loved Angela's questions, loved the way she didn't settle for easy answers.

"We've never tried. But right now, it's something both of us are thinking hard about." He paused. "Does it bother you, what I am?"

She shook her head. "Even now, as we're sitting here talking about it, I don't really think of you as a host. You're just Tomas to me."

"Do you mind if I ask you something else?" Tomas asked. "Something more personal?"

"Not at all."

"You have every reason to hate me," he said. "We fought on opposite sides, and you know enough about me to know what I did. And you've never even blinked at it. Why?"

Angela thought about her answer for a few moments. "I believe that too many people look at the wrong things when they judge someone else. You're right. I could look at you and see an enemy soldier, one no doubt responsible for a tremendous amount of suffering among people I considered friends and allies. I could see you as a host, an unnatural abomination that deserves to be wiped off the face of the planet. Hells, I could look at Ben and see nothing more than an inquisitor."

She leaned forward, warming to her subject. "And all those ideas would be true and defensible, but I've been a marshal here for years, and was an officer for many years prior to that, and if there's one thing I know, it's that people shouldn't be so easily labeled. You've fought when you didn't have to. You've saved my life several times, though I was a very effective commander for the other side. I've seen you hold back when you didn't have to. And so all the words I could use to describe you don't matter. I know who you are."

She left Tomas speechless.

For years, now, he'd had an understanding with Elzeth that was impossible to describe to others. The two of them were almost literally inseparable, and it forced them to find ways to live together. They had no other choice. But after years of being together, Tomas' relationship with Elzeth was the cornerstone of his very existence.

For the first time, he had a glimpse of what that type of relationship might look like with another person.

He almost shuddered at the thought.

"You're one of the most remarkable people I've ever met," he said.

"Damn straight," she replied.

He laughed, and she stood. "I'm going to get a bottle of wine, and I fully expect you to help me finish it."

"Yes, ma'am."

They finished that bottle, and then another, and it was possibly the best night Tomas had ever had in his life.

But in the morning, reality intruded once again. Her deputy came with news. One of the caravans scheduled to arrive in the next day or two wasn't what it first seemed. It was one run by the Family.

33

The dust from the approaching caravans hung like a motionless cloud in the sky. Somehow, the sun had found a way to heat the air even more than it already was. It wasn't even close to noon yet, and already Tomas' shirt was sticking to his back.

Lying motionless on the roof of a shop did him no favors, either. Vance, one of Angela's two surviving and healthy deputies, was prone beside him, studying the approaching caravan over the barrel of Angela's rifle.

Below, Angela and Russ, her final deputy, stood in the center of the east-west main street. A smile played at the edges of Tomas' mouth as he remembered his own welcome to Razin.

The caravan was longer than Tomas expected. He encountered caravans often enough, but farther west, they were rarely more than four or five wagons. This one, Tomas had stopped counting after he hit thirty. "Is that more wagons than usual?" he asked.

Vance grunted. "Middle of the pack. Our biggest ones usually arrive in the spring."

Tomas shook his head. He imagined the flow of trade, all coming here, then branching out in a dozen different directions. He understood now why Angela hired as many deputies as she had.

She looked small down there, standing against the long line of carts and wagons. But she didn't so much as shift her weight from foot to foot. She guarded her town as protectively as any stone wall.

A remarkable woman.

In more ways than one.

The caravan ground to a halt some ways before it reached the marshal. A group of riders casually assembled near the front of the caravan. Tomas watched but saw no signs of tension or worry. The whole scene had the feeling of a ritual, a dance performed every time a caravan arrived at the outskirts of town.

Once assembled, the riders advanced at an easy canter. They reached Angela and dismounted. Bows were exchanged, all of them of appropriate depth. If there was anything amiss, Tomas couldn't spot it. Though Angela assured him Family would be present, Tomas couldn't say who among the caravan's spokespeople it was. The dust from the road obscured any subtle differences he might have otherwise observed. From where he lay, they all looked like little more than weary travelers.

They spoke for a few minutes, and then there was another round of bowing. The ritual was complete. The riders mounted their horses and returned to the caravan. Angela turned also and met Tomas' gaze. She gave him a quick nod, then made her way toward the market square. There, she would observe the caravans as they set up their shops.

It would be a busy day in Razin. The giant, invisible hands of commerce turned forever forward.

Vance sighed and flipped the sight down on the rifle. "Looks like they won't try anything yet."

Angela hadn't thought they would. It was possible the Family that had just arrived didn't yet know their outpost had been raided. But whether they knew or not, Angela assumed they would wait until they were firmly established in town to act.

It was always easier to conquer a land when you were already on it.

Vance wiggled to breathe life into limbs he'd held too still for too long. He pushed himself to his feet and slung the rifle over his shoulder. "Get some rest," the deputy said. "You'll need it."

"Good luck today," Tomas replied.

Vance tipped his hat and went to the edge of the roof, where they'd positioned a ladder. Within moments he was gone.

Tomas watched the caravan for a couple more minutes but didn't see anything particularly concerning.

He followed Vance off the roof, preferring alleys to streets as he made his way back to Angela's place. Once she'd done enough to be visible to the caravans as they settled, she would join him.

When tonight came, they'd be ready.

He was fixing lunch when she arrived. Her exhaustion left bags under her eyes, but she smiled when she entered. She inhaled deeply, appreciating the scents of his cooking. "Better be careful," she warned. "If you're going to keep cooking me meals, I might just extend my invitation for longer."

He placed the plate in front of her. "Consider me warned."

She devoured half her plate before speaking again. "They're not even pretending. None of the Family even went looking for Callum's inn, where they usually stay. They went straight to the mission."

Tomas almost choked on his food.

"That was about my reaction, as well," she said.

Once Tomas safely swallowed his food, he considered the implications. In his experience, the Family and the church had fought because they wanted control over the same resources. Was this alliance unique to Razin, or did it represent a nationwide shift?

He tapped his fingers on Angela's table.

It didn't matter, really. Here, the factions were working together. That was all he needed to know.

When they finished their meal, he took the plates from the table to the sink. She came up behind him as he worked and wrapped her arms around his waist. With a grin, he turned around, and for the rest of the morning, they forgot the world outside and all its troubles.

They slept after, the light from the sun crawling across Angela's bedroom.

Tomas woke first. He lay there, Angela's hair tickling his cheek. Her back was snuggled up against his torso, and he felt her soft breath against his arm. He breathed deeply, willing himself to remember this moment for as long as he lived.

"Have you thought about after?" Elzeth asked. The sagani was so tranquil, Tomas had barely felt him stir.

"A lot," Tomas said, "and not nearly enough."

"Would you stay if she asked?"

Tomas tilted his head so he could see her better. Razin

had too many people and felt too crowded and busy. But when he thought of Angela, none of those facts bothered him like they usually did. He felt comfortable here. Understood.

Such a relationship was not to be taken lightly.

And yet, the idea of settling here and now made him uneasy. Perhaps it was an instinct he needed to listen to, or it was just his inability to acknowledge his own fear of finding peace.

A hundred philosophers could debate that until the end of days, and still not have an answer.

Finally, he answered Elzeth's question, as best as he could. "I don't know. You have an opinion?"

Elzeth didn't answer for so long Tomas thought he'd fallen asleep. But when he spoke, his voice was firm. "Were it up to me alone, I believe I'd stay."

For as well as he knew Elzeth, the answer surprised Tomas. "You don't care if we ever learn the answers about what's happening to us?"

"I think Ben has the right of it," Elzeth said. "It doesn't matter. We're healthy and stronger than we've ever been. Why waste the time wandering for answers that may not even exist?"

Tomas stared up at the ceiling. "I guess it's a question we'll have to answer if we survive this."

Elzeth knew Tomas was putting off the question, but he didn't push the matter.

A knock on the front door woke Angela up. She glanced out the window at the setting sun, then grinned at him. She dressed quickly and went to answer the door. Tomas used Elzeth to listen from the bedroom.

It was Vance. "Family's on the move. They've been leaving in twos and threes from the mission for the last fifteen minutes or so. Near as we can tell, they're spreading out through the town."

"Take cover in the jail."

Tomas could hear the hesitation in the answering silence. "Doesn't seem right, leaving this to you."

"I'll find Tomas," Angela said. "He'll help. But I'm not losing any more deputies. The jail is the easiest place to defend. And don't worry, they'll come for you. You'll see plenty of action tonight."

Eventually, Vance left, although he still didn't seem happy about the arrangements. By the time Angela returned, Tomas was dressed and ready for the night.

"You heard?" she asked.

"I'd feel better if you were with them," he said.

"I'm not going to hide while they try to take over my town." The determination in her voice left no room for argument.

"Be safe, then," Tomas said.

"You, too." She came closer, and Tomas kissed her.

He left then, from the back exit. He slipped into the lengthening shadows of dusk, ready for the battle to begin.

34

The air, so still for the past few days, now blew steadily from the west. At times, it gusted hard enough to bend some of the taller trees. Perched on the edge of a roof, Tomas looked to the horizon. Tolkin would rise tonight, as it always did, but it would cast no illumination on the battle below. Thick, angry storm clouds built in the distance. Lightning flickered, brief flashes of jagged light that left afterimages in his vision. The thunder from the flashes was constant, a low rumble near the limit of his hearing.

As he watched, the storm grew larger, encompassing more of the horizon. It wouldn't be long before the rain hit.

Tomas enjoyed the sight a moment longer. He loved the power and ferocity of a storm on the plains. It made him feel small. It reminded him that for all his strength, there were forces on this planet far larger than him. His life, in the grand arc of history, meant little.

He supposed some might feel depressed by such a realization, but it never failed to bring him some measure of peace.

Tonight, though, there would be no peace. Instead of watching the storm arrive, he would use it as cover against the Family even now moving throughout Razin.

He'd traveled by rooftops and alleys, using his heightened senses to avoid confrontation until it best suited him. But he heard them moving, keeping to the alleys and shadows, like rats in an enormous maze.

What, exactly, they planned, Tomas couldn't say.

Nor did he particularly care. He wasn't the law, beholden to an ethos of reaction. They were Family, aligned with the church. He would end them all and not feel so much as a pang of guilt. Surely, the sniper had felt none that first night when he'd killed Robick.

He leaped lightly from one rooftop to the next, listening for any of the small groups of Family that wandered the town.

A soft rain started to fall as he jumped across another alley. The wind picked up, as though trying to make up for the days it had stood motionless. Lightning cut across the sky, scattering in all directions through the clouds.

A moment later, the sky opened up. In only a few moments, Tomas was soaked, his clothes dripping. Thunder cracked and boomed, loud enough he could feel it through his feet, and he was forced to give up Elzeth's hearing.

Tomas continued toward the jail. Whatever the Family planned, he was certain it would be involved.

Two alleys later, Tomas' suspicion was rewarded. Two men were huddling over something small, trying to protect it from the rain. Lightning flashed, and Tomas clearly saw the tattoos on their arms marking them as Family.

In most places, those tattoos would afford them protection. Tonight, it made them targets.

Tomas glanced around to ensure they weren't being

observed. When the next thunder rolled overhead, Tomas stepped off the roof.

He landed easily.

They never noticed him. Two cuts created two corpses, and Tomas squatted down to see what had so attracted their attention. It was a small barrel with a fuse.

"Hells," Tomas said.

They were only a few buildings away from the jail. Tomas suspected that was the Family's intended destination, at least for this barrel. He walked to the end of the alley and poked his head around the corner, cursing again at what he saw.

The street was filled with shadowy wraiths, darting from whatever shelter they could find from the rain. They ran toward the jail, some carrying barrels with lit fuses.

The first gunshot came from Tomas' left. One of the Family was punched backward, as though hit in the chest with an enormous hammer.

Tomas twisted his neck to see Angela several buildings down, a wide-brimmed hat protecting her face from the rain. The barrel of her rifle smoked, but she calmly cycled the lever action, kicking out the spent casing and loading another round.

Several Family charged her, but more continued their advance on the jail.

Tomas waited for a moment. His gut was twisting, not from fear, but from a recognition that something was not as it should be. But what?

He gave the fight another precious few seconds to develop, but the battle appeared to be nothing more than it was. Angela shot again, dropping a second Family as she charged. Angela pumped the lever, though Tomas wasn't sure she'd get a third shot off before she had to switch to a sword.

Finally, he could wait no longer.

Elzeth flared to life, so bright Tomas glanced down at his arms, convinced he would glow. He dashed across the street, intercepting one of the pairs carrying a barrel. The escort had his sword out but was too slow to block Tomas' cut. He fell with a cry.

The man carrying the barrel skidded to a stop, holding the powder between them as though it was a shield. Tomas cut, slicing the fuse below where it burned. Tomas saw the man watch the fuse spin away and into the mud. His eyes went wide, and his mouth formed a curse, but before he could finish uttering it, Tomas drove his sword deep through the man's stomach.

He pulled it out as the man fell.

A shout gave him just enough warning to slide to the side as a woman cut through the air where he'd just been standing. She spun but lost her balance in the mud of the street.

Tomas couldn't attack her, though. Two other Family followed her, and they'd fought together before. They launched a dizzying storm of steel in his direction, and he gave up ground to avoid being flayed alive.

The wind whipped down the street, racing from one end of town to the other. Rain stung Tomas' eyes as he kept his vitals away from the sharp steel.

Angela fired again, the sound barely indistinguishable from the thunder above.

The woman who'd charged past Tomas recovered her balance and attacked him from behind. He spun away, only to find himself face-to-face against all three warriors. Behind his assailants, other Family members had placed their small barrels against the jail walls and were running away.

"Get out of there!" Tomas bellowed, hoping the deputies inside would hear him.

He didn't have time for anything else as the trio of Family advanced.

Tomas felt time slip as Elzeth burned even brighter. Tomas chose the woman on his left, the one who'd first attacked him. He stepped toward her, turning aside her cut, stepping inside her guard, and cutting her from neck to hip.

Then he heard, rather than saw, the attack aimed at the back of his neck. He bent his legs and looked down, listening to the blade as it passed over the back of his head. He stabbed back with his sword, trusting his judgment. The weapon scraped against bone, but the grunt of pain told him he'd bought at least a moment.

At the jail, the front door burst open, and the two remaining deputies poked their heads out.

"Run!" Tomas yelled. Then he retreated again as the third Family stabbed at him.

It was enough. The deputies ran.

They'd only made it about a dozen steps, though, when the bombs exploded.

35

The blasts rocked Tomas back, but he kept his feet underneath him. Anyone too close to the jail was picked up by giant invisible hands and tossed, bodies cartwheeling through the air. Tomas shut his eyes and turned his head away as shards of debris cut through the air.

His ears rang and eyes watered.

For one long breath, the jail stood, defiantly shrugging off the attack that blew enormous holes in its sides. Then it groaned, even its sturdy walls pushed beyond their limits.

The building twisted and collapsed, the sound almost as loud as the explosions. A cloud of dust billowed out, only to be blown away by the wind and decimated by the torrential rain.

Movement caught his eye, over by Angela.

The marshal was frozen, eyes focused on the deputies lying motionless in the street. She didn't see the shadows gathering behind her, emerging from the alleys like vengeful wraiths. Tomas ignored the Family beside him and sprinted toward her. One of the Family chased him, close behind.

The sharp crack of a rifle behind him overwhelmed the sound of the rolling thunder. The Family chasing Tomas fell, blood blooming across his shirt.

Tomas twisted and saw a familiar figure, rifle pointed in his direction. The lever action cycled too quickly for a mere human.

Of course, the host would be here.

As the shadows converged behind Angela, Tomas understood the Family had been prepared for just this battle. They lured Tomas and his allies in with the assault on the jail, then wrapped the noose tight around their necks.

Angela's shock only lasted a few moments. She tore her stare away from the deputies and saw him running for her. She looked behind her, saw the Family advancing, and dropped her rifle as her hand went for her sword.

He couldn't fight the host and assist Angela. They were too far apart.

He was surprised how easy the decision was.

He weaved left and right as he ran, and no more shots came from behind him.

Angela's sword cleared its sheath as he passed her.

Then he was among the Family.

They'd been prepared, but not enough. Bodies fell into the mud as he passed. He cleared a path, then turned and entered the fray again.

More gunshots boomed from down the street, but Tomas and Angela were surrounded by a wall of Family. Tomas didn't hear any bullets pass by. Had the host even been firing at them?

Before he could reach her, she fell to her knees, blood pouring from a cut on her side.

One swordsman stood between them, his back to Tomas as he raised his sword to finish Angela. Tomas stabbed out with his blade, the point punching through the man's back and out the front of his chest. He planted his feet firmly and twisted, lifting the man off the ground and throwing him into one of his compatriots. Tomas' sword came free, and he stepped forward to protect Angela.

Numbers thinning, the Family swords all closed in on him at once. Their swords sought any part of him to cut, but the best any could do was a shallow cut across his arm. Despite their numerical advantage, it wasn't the swords that worried him.

It was the host, waiting for a clear shot.

Angela fought her way back to her feet, water pouring from her hat. Pain was etched in every line of her face, but her sword came up and she dueled the first man who dared attack her. Tomas kept himself in position to guard her back, allowing her to fight one enemy at a time.

In the distance, the host waited, barrel trained on Tomas. The Family between them wanted to kill Tomas, but they also kept him alive.

Tomas' sword cut through the rain, flinging blood and water in equal measure. When lightning flashed, his blade appeared to stand still for a moment.

Another boom shook the air. Not thunder, nor a rifle.

More black powder?

Tomas had no time to find the source of the explosion. The Family, to their credit, never surrendered even as their numbers dwindled. They fought on, until the last warrior fell to Tomas' blade. As soon as she did, Tomas spun, grabbed Angela, and dove.

The host fired, the bullet passing overhead.

Tomas tried to run, but the blood and water had mixed

in with the dirt of the street, creating a muddy mess that prevented his feet from gaining meaningful traction. He lunged, still holding Angela, as a bullet threw up mud in front of his face.

He couldn't get them both to safety.

Tomas let go of Angela and half-leaped, half-crawled as the rifle boomed again. He didn't feel any impact, and he hoped the bullet hadn't hit Angela.

He got his feet under him and ran, finding firmer ground closer to the buildings along the side of the street.

Tomas sprinted, legs churning, and the host tracked him with the rifle. Tomas just couldn't move fast enough to evade the host's reflexes. Had he started closer, it might have been a different story.

A rifle boomed from behind him, and just for a moment, the host's eyes weren't on Tomas. The barrel fell a step behind.

Tomas shouted and put all his energy into his legs. The host's focus returned to Tomas, and the barrel caught up to him again. Tomas leaped as the host pulled the trigger.

He avoided the bullet, but the host slid smoothly to the side as Tomas passed by him. The host dropped the rifle and drew his sword, and Tomas finally got the opportunity he'd been waiting for. They crossed swords on equal footing, and Tomas found the host wanting.

Two passes cut the man down.

Tomas snarled. His blood boiled, and he swore the rain steamed as it hit his arms.

There were no more foes, yet he was not satisfied. The Family needed to suffer more for what they had helped perpetrate.

Down the street, Angela twisted and fell. Her hat rolled off her head, stopping upside down in the mud. The sight broke Tomas' anger, and he ran toward her. She was clutching at her side, gasping as the rain fell hard against her face. "Angela!"

She grimaced as he kneeled in the mud next to her. "Forgot how much that hurts. Take me to Vance and Russ."

In the heat of the battle, Tomas had forgotten completely about the deputies. But now wasn't the time. "You need a doctor."

Her glare was answer enough. He bit back his reply and helped her to her feet. He supported most of her weight, and together they shuffled over to the deputies.

Tomas could guess their fate even from a distance. They were too still, and there was too much blood pooled around them. No enemies had fallen nearby, though.

The mystery was solved as they got closer. Both had bullet wounds in their heads.

The extra shots from the host, while Tomas and Angela had been fighting the rest of the Family.

He'd killed them while they were already down, injured from the explosion.

Tomas' rage reignited, and Elzeth had no choice but to respond, burning even brighter. The barriers that separated them burned in the fires of Tomas' anger.

"Woah," Elzeth said, trying to calm Tomas as though he were a wild horse.

That host deserved to die a much slower, much more painful death.

Angela's legs gave out when she realized what had happened. Tomas caught her and held her tight. Her body convulsed, but her cries were silent against the thunderous storm.

Lightning stuck somewhere nearby, and a fresh wave of thunder rolled overhead.

The sound made him think of the explosion, somewhere off in the distance. He looked around, but beside the jail, nothing else was damaged or destroyed.

"Did you hear the explosion?" Tomas asked Angela.

She glanced up, her eyes blank. "What explosion?"

"There was another explosion in the middle of the fight." He thought back to the way the shadows had detached from the walls. How they'd been ready. How this had been planned. His stomach sank. "I need to go," he said.

Doubt flickered in Angela's eyes, but then she nodded. "I'll come with you."

She swore at the look he gave her. "It's still my town. So, help me."

Tomas picked her up in his arms. With Elzeth burning as bright as he was, it was no more difficult than picking up a small sack of potatoes.

He ran toward the source of the sound, glancing left and right for signs of another explosion.

His worst fears were confirmed when he turned a corner and saw Ben's place.

For the first time since Tomas had come to Razin, the place was quiet. A hole had been blown in the wall, and Tomas saw no movement in the yard beyond.

36

Tomas ran with Angela to the hole in the wall. He peered in, but the yard was as silent as a cemetery. He set Angela down on her feet. The marshal leaned up against the wall, still clutching her side. But she wouldn't seek help, not until her sense of duty was satisfied. "I'm going in," he said.

She didn't try to follow. "I might sit this one out."

He drew his sword and stepped through the hole.

The yard near the blast site was a mess of debris and muddy footprints. A lot of people had gone through the gap, and recently.

There were bodies here, too. Four of them, all bearing wounds that were becoming all too familiar. They had no identifying tattoos, so they weren't Family. Considering the circumstances, that probably made them believers. Against Ben, they'd had no chance. The former inquisitor's cuts had been precise and lethal.

But where was Ben? Or the children?

He remained silent as he approached the house. It was dark, the windows shuttered against the storm. Above him, the trees swayed in the wind, one of the larger oaks creaking as it danced back and forth. Small branches, torn off the tree by the gale, spun madly as the currents of air in the yard caught them.

The front door of the house had been broken open. It swung back and forth on one hinge, slamming repeatedly into the frame. Tomas caught the door and shouted. "Ben? Olena? Anyone?"

If there was a response, it was too quiet for him to hear over the wind and the thunder.

He stepped into the house. He trailed water and mud inside, but a glance at the floor told him he hadn't been the first.

Tomas stepped cautiously, letting his ears warn him of any dangers. In between strikes of lightning and the accompanying thunder, he thought he heard something, coming from the back of the house.

"Ben? Olena?" He listened but heard nothing. "It's Tomas. Is anyone here?"

He passed one bedroom and then another. Unlike his previous visit, none of the beds were made. They were all empty. From the general disorder, it looked like many of the kids had been forcibly pulled from them.

Tomas' grip tightened on his sword until his knuckles were white. He sheathed it, before it became a problem.

Again, he thought he heard something from farther back. High-pitched, and almost whiny.

It sounded like it was coming from Ben's study.

He checked all the bedrooms in between. The children might be injured, or worse. But they were all empty, and soon he found himself in front of Ben's study. "Ben?"

He knocked, and the door was pulled inward, so fast Tomas almost fell forward.

He caught sight of a knife aimed at his chest. Olena followed behind it, eyes wide with fear and madness.

Tomas easily deflected the knife and caught hold of Olena.

She struggled, and Tomas shook her until she looked up at him. Recognition was slow in coming, but once it did, she went limp in his arms. He guided her to the floor and looked around.

Some of the kids were here, huddled in the corner of the room, scrawny arms around one another.

Tomas looked to Olena. "What happened here?"

When she didn't respond, he stood up. The children were safe, at least for the moment. At least the ones that were here. There weren't enough, though. He did a quick count and realized almost half of them were missing. Including Clara.

He turned his attention back to Ben's wife. "Olena. What happened?"

Perhaps it was the tone of his voice, or perhaps she'd finally had enough time to gather her wits. Either way, she answered. "They came for us, and he froze!"

Tomas frowned, not understanding. "Slow down, Olena. Tell me what happened."

She took several deep breaths, then tried again. "We heard the explosions from town, and Ben said they were attacking. We hid inside the house. Then the wall blew in!"

Her eyes darted around the room, and Tomas feared she would slip back into shock. But she held onto her reason. She continued. "I thought Ben would fight. He was ready to fight. But when the men came through the wall he froze. It was like he couldn't move. One of them hit him over the top of the head and he was out."

Tomas squatted so he was closer to her level. He couldn't

imagine what would cause Ben to behave in such a way, and he didn't much want to think about it. He reached out and held her hands steady in his. "Then what happened?"

"They took them. They threw them in a cart, and they left."

Tomas thought to the bodies in the yard. He could guess then what had happened. "Ben came to, didn't he?"

She nodded. "They had loaded up the first cart and it left. They had a second cart and meant to take us, too. But Ben came to, and he fought like nothing I'd ever seen before."

There'd been no carts out in front of the place. Tomas was sure enough of that. "Ben chased them."

"He told us to stay here, and that he would be back once he rescued the others."

Tomas stood and cursed to himself. He didn't doubt Ben's competence, but he wasn't young anymore. And he'd already frozen once. The inquisitor had seen something terrifying enough to cause him to falter. The odds of him successfully rescuing the children didn't seem good.

Clara's face floated through his thoughts. Kind and curious. Despite a life that had brought her into Ben and Olena's care.

His nostrils flared, and he struggled to control his breathing. The barriers between him and Elzeth began to burn at the edges. "Stay here," he said. "Just in the house. No need to hide in the study." The room they were in didn't matter. Ben had already guaranteed that much.

Tomas spun on his heel and stomped out the door before Olena could ask a single question.

Angela stopped him as he stepped out of the hole in the wall. "Tomas?"

He couldn't look at her, his eyes already searching for

the track of the carts. They were easy to find in the rain. "Go into the home," Tomas said. "Olena can wash and bandage your wound."

"What happened? What are you going to do?" She reached out and grabbed his arm. He heard the concern in her voice like a distant cry.

"They took the children," Tomas said. He looked down at her and their eyes met. She flinched away, but still held onto his arm. She searched for answers in his gaze and nodded when she found them.

She squeezed his arm, then let go. "Kill them all, then." She stepped away.

"I intend to."

37

Tomas followed the cart tracks out of Razin on foot. The rain and mud simplified the task, and before long he found himself a half mile out of town. So long as the tracks were clear, he kept a steady pace, eating up the distance with ease.

As he ran, the storm moved on. The rain eased, feeling less like bullets falling from the sky. Thunder still rolled across the plains, but it was farther east now. Lightning tickled the horizon instead of splitting the air overhead.

The thoughts that had troubled him for days were gone, burned to ash in the fire of his anger. His full attention went to the task of tracking the kidnapped children.

No words passed between him and Elzeth. The sagani burned bright, the last shreds of identity that separated them little more than a thin, transparent veil.

Not unity, but so close it almost didn't matter. Elzeth was in his bones, his muscles, and his heart. They needed no words, their thoughts beating in tandem. Tomas' rage was Elzeth's, and for once, there was no debate about what needed to be done.

A small voice of concern called out for notice, but Tomas and Elzeth smothered it. They knew what it was and what it would say. It was Tomas' reason, arguing that they'd never burned so bright for so long.

It reminded them of the cost of such power. The destiny of a host.

Tomas snarled and ignored it.

A flash of lightning illuminated a horse-pulled cart, perhaps a quarter mile away. At first glance, it appeared empty, and Tomas ran faster toward it.

He almost tripped over a body. He glanced down but didn't recognize the woman's face. The cuts that had killed her were familiar enough, though.

Ben's work.

He slowed down as he approached the cart, the sound of labored breathing warning him that he wasn't alone. As he walked around the cart, he found the source.

Ben leaned against the wheel of the cart, holding tight to his side. Several cuts decorated his body, and they were eerily familiar. Tomas didn't think he'd ever see them on Ben, though. They were cuts from an inquisitor's weapon.

Ben saw Tomas and forced a bloody smile onto his face. "Thought you might be along."

Tomas heard the older man's heart pounding in his body. Though the inquisitor struggled for breath, Tomas didn't hear any sound of a punctured or collapsed lung. "Fatal?"

Ben grimaced. "Tough to say. Bad, regardless."

"Where did they go?"

"They're still in the cart. You can follow them."

Tomas turned to leave, but Ben's voice stopped him. "Is this unity?"

Tomas turned back. "No, but close."

"How long have you been burning?"

"Since the explosions at the jail."

Ben nodded, and Tomas was about to leave him again when he spoke. "Their inquisitor is good."

Tomas saw Ben was struggling to hold onto consciousness. His eyes fluttered, as though he were exhausted. "If I succeed, I'll come back for you."

Ben gritted his teeth. "I know. Not..." His voice trailed off as his eyes closed. He muttered quietly under his breath, and if not for Elzeth, Tomas wouldn't have heard. "Not what you need to know."

Then he was out.

Tomas debated for a moment, then stood. He imagined the secret was what had frozen Ben back in his place. But it hadn't stopped Ben from giving chase, nor had it had anything to do with Ben's defeat. That was an inquisitor's work, but it didn't matter how talented an inquisitor was. They were nothing compared to a host. Whatever the secret, it wasn't worth the time Tomas would waste discovering it.

He resumed tracking the cart, a task that was still easy. It followed a path Tomas was well familiar with. It led to the farmhouse where the Family had posted their guards.

Tomas swore. After all that, had he somehow missed something? Were the kids in danger because he had failed?

It couldn't be. He'd checked the farmhouse several times, as had Angela. Nothing could have escaped their notice.

But as he followed the tracks, it became abundantly clear there could be only one destination.

Soon enough, the farmhouse once again came into view. The windows were dark, and the barn doors were closed. Except for the cart sitting outside the barn, the place could have been exactly as Tomas had left it a few days ago.

The cart was manned by a person Tomas recognized. It was the priest Devon, turning the cart around to bring it back to Razin.

Had that been Ben's news? It seemed a small detail.

Regardless, Tomas looked forward to their conversation. He didn't bother trying to hide. Devon was no fighter. He ran as quickly as he could, covering the last of the distance to the barn in less than a minute. Devon wasn't even paying attention to his surroundings. By the time he noticed Tomas, he barely had time to utter a surprised cry.

Tomas leaped up, leading with his knee. He caught Devon in the chest, and together they landed in the bed of the cart. Tomas took hold of Devon's hair in one hand and slammed the priest's head into the cart. His eyes went dazed, and Tomas pulled him close, until their noses were almost touching. "Where are they?"

Devon recovered his wits more quickly than Tomas expected. He smirked. "I'll never tell a demon like you."

Tomas stood, pulling the man to his feet. He tossed Devon over the side of the cart. He landed awkwardly, and he fell as Tomas heard one of the bones in his leg snap.

He groaned, but didn't scream. Tomas vaulted over the edge of the cart and landed softly on his feet. Devon made no move to run away.

"Where are they?" Tomas asked.

Devon grinned, his eyes dancing with joy. "I'll never tell you!"

Tomas drove the toe of his boot into the man's stomach. When that didn't work, he kicked him in the face. His only reward was a mad giggle.

Hell cursed believers.

Tomas didn't have time. Every breath those children took in the presence of their captors was one breath too many. He drew his sword and let Devon drink in the sight of its edge. "Last chance," he said.

Devon just giggled again.

Tomas stabbed him in the leg.

Devon groaned, but the ecstasy in his eyes never faded.

"The next one will hurt far worse," Tomas said. "Tell me where they are."

"I suffer in the name of the holy water, which offers eternal life," Devon answered.

Tomas stabbed him in the stomach. Devon screamed, but offered no answers.

The cut was fatal, although it would take some time. Time Devon would spend in agony.

"Tell me," Tomas said.

Devon spoke, but his words were those of the church's daily prayer.

Tomas almost left him there. It would have been repayment enough for the crimes Devon had been a part of. It would have felt just.

Tomas cut once, and Devon's prayers went silent.

The children were close. He just had to find them.

He followed the tracks of the cart to where it had been parked. There were footsteps. Lots of them, fresh in the mud.

Even better, there was blood.

Perhaps Ben had left another member of the church party injured. It was a far more optimistic thought than the other possibility, that one of the children had been injured.

Tomas followed the trail but began to struggle once the grass and wheat grew tall around him. The clouds still obscured the moon, giving Tomas little light to work by. The grass had been well trampled in different places, too, making tracking nearly impossible.

He followed the blood.

It led him true, and soon he was a few hundred feet behind the farm, somewhere near where Angela might have been the night they assaulted the place. He came upon a small tube, sticking out of the ground. He found another a dozen paces later. In the wide fields, it would have been a miracle to find them. Then, after another dozen paces, he found a trapdoor in the middle of the field.

It was a small thing, no more than two feet to a side. It was farther away from the house than they'd searched, and even if they had gone out this far, a person essentially had to step on it to find it. Tomas lifted the trapdoor. A chute went straight down, a thin metal ladder providing access. Light flickered at the bottom.

He heard children crying and screaming. Then a door shut, the chute went dark, and it was as silent as though Tomas was all alone in the world.

Tomas swore. The answers had been so close, all this time.

He swung his leg over and climbed down the ladder into the darkness below.

38

A t the bottom of the ladder, Tomas had to feel with his hands to find the door. Fortunately, in the tight space, there wasn't much to search. He found the latch with little difficulty. He opened the door.

The inside was almost blindingly bright, lit by lanterns that left no place for shadows to hide. Crates of supplies, similar to those in the barn above, were stacked in every corner. Tomas walked quietly through the room to another door that was partway open. He peeked through the crack, and his breath caught in his throat. There were two cells, the doors made of thick metal bars. The children from Ben's place had all been stuffed into one, so tight they barely fit.

No one else was in the room. Another door was closed tightly on the other side. Tomas entered, putting a finger to his lips to silence the children when they saw him. A quick glance told him that only the younger children were in the cell. A few of the older ones, like Clara, weren't here.

He squatted down next to the bars. "Is anyone hurt?"

The children all shook their heads.

"What about the others? The children who aren't here. Were they hurt?"

One of the boys spoke up. "No."

That was good news, at least. The amount of blood that had been spilled out in the field was enough to kill a child. It meant that his guess had been correct. Ben had injured one of the kidnappers.

"Did they go that way?" Tomas pointed toward the closed door. The children nodded.

Tomas looked around the room, but there was no key hanging on the wall, nor any way he could see of actually breaking the cell doors open. Strong as he was with Elzeth, even he couldn't bend metal this thick.

"I'm going to follow them," Tomas said. He shushed the whimpers from the children. "I need you to be quiet. Once I find them, I'll come back with the keys, and we'll all go back to Ben's together."

The children nodded, tears streaming from several young faces.

Tomas stood, doing his best to ignore the cries. "I'll be back in a few minutes," he said. "Just wait for me."

He went to the door and waited a moment for the crying to quiet. Then he opened the next door.

The sight froze him in his tracks.

The main features of the small room were two thick tables, about six feet long and three feet wide. They looked to be made from railroad ties and must have weighed several hundred pounds each.

Both tables had straps built into them.

Along one wall, a cabinet with a glass door displayed dozens of bottles, filled with liquids of various colors. Another table, smaller, contained surgical implements.

The room wasn't empty. A man sat on one table,

bleeding from several cuts to his arms and torso. A woman stood beside him, her attention consumed by one of the cuts she was stitching.

Tomas noted them in a heartbeat, but his attention was focused mostly on the other table.

One of Ben's older boys lay there, naked, eyes closed, a cloth gag in his mouth. His chest rose softly, but other than that, he looked like the dead. His arms and legs were tightly strapped down to the table, so tight his hands and feet were beginning to turn purple.

It took Tomas a full two seconds to understand that what he was seeing was real. That this was happening and not some nightmare.

He'd never had any love for the church.

But this, this was beyond any forgiveness.

The delay cost Tomas dearly, though.

The man being operated on saw Tomas and shouted, the warning echoing in the small rooms and further down the hall.

Tomas leaped forward.

He cut at the woman first, killing her before she'd even had time to turn around. The man scrambled backward, but he, too, fell to a single cut. Neither of them had been warriors.

Not that he cared. Anyone involved with this place deserved any fate coming to them.

There was a commotion further down the hall. Someone was shouting, a familiar voice that Tomas took a moment to place. It was the same voice that had once bribed a roomful of mercenaries to kill Tomas as he slept. The mysterious stranger was close, too.

From the sound of it, he was in charge here.

Tomas grinned viciously.

There was the clang of a heavy door, and then it was quiet.

Tomas glanced down at the boy, unconscious on the table. With his sword, he cut the leather restraints. When he returned, he'd be able to do more.

For now, there was work to be done.

Tomas continued deeper into the complex.

The next room felt distinctly out of place after all that he had seen. A small table sat in the center with four chairs around it. One door, to Tomas' left, was open to a small bunk room with four beds inside.

The only other door, to Tomas' right, was open just a crack. He peered in.

It was different than any other room he'd seen yet. The others had been square, built and reinforced mostly with wood. This was a long tunnel, a cylinder made of metal, barely large enough for him to stand in.

"Come on in," said the man standing on the opposite side of the hallway. A collection of switches was on the wall behind him, next to the door.

Tomas recognized the other inquisitor. His nose still looked out of sorts from when Tomas had broken it.

Of course, it was a trap.

But what did he have to fear? He and Elzeth were still so close to unity no one could beat them, not even a skilled inquisitor. And besides, Tomas still hadn't found all the children or the key. The only way was forward.

He opened the door.

He didn't give the inquisitor any chance. There was no point in talking, no questions he wanted the inquisitor to answer. As soon as the door was open, he charged forward, leading with his sword.

The inquisitor smiled and reached out with his left hand. He carried no weapon.

Instead, he grabbed the biggest switch on the wall behind him and flipped it up.

The whole room hummed, and Tomas' sword was ripped from his hand.

His legs suddenly turned to jam, and as he fell forward, he realized, with a sickening horror, what had happened.

Elzeth was gone.

39

Some things in life were as good as certain.

The sun rose from its slumber every morning in the east. Tolkin and Shen walked a similar path every night. Lightning brought thunder close behind.

For almost as many years as he could remember, Tomas had known that Elzeth would always be with him, a comforting presence in the pit of his stomach. Until recently, they always assumed the death of one would be the death of the other. Even the final journey to the gates wouldn't separate them.

So, Elzeth's sudden disappearance hit Tomas harder than a brick to the face.

It was as if a hole opened in the center of his stomach, swallowing everything.

His limbs, once full of energy, turned to water. His thoughts, once sharp and crisp, became as muddy as the trail outside. A moment ago, he'd been alert. But now, he was exhausted.

He'd been burning all night. He'd battled outside the jail, then run all the way here. Until the inquisitor flipped that switch, Elzeth had been masking the inhuman effort Tomas had sustained.

He caught himself on his hands as he fell, belatedly remembering he had no sword. It was held against the wall of the tube by no force that Tomas understood.

He felt violently sick, as though his stomach wanted to expel everything he'd ever eaten and everything he ever would eat. He dry-heaved once, his eyes watering. His head buzzed, a thousand bees angry that their nest had been disturbed.

The inquisitor laughed but wasn't so foolish as to waste his advantage. He drew a dark knife from his hip, and Tomas stared at it, his sluggish mind trying to understand why the inquisitor got a weapon and he didn't.

He recognized the blade then. Obsidian, knapped to a sharp edge.

A veritable menagerie of thoughts tumbled through his mind. Ben had called the inquisitor skilled. Despite growing older, Ben had been no slouch with his own weapon, and he'd been left for dead. This man didn't have a cut on him. And Tomas wasn't sure if he was a host any longer.

He pushed himself up, but before he even found his feet, the inquisitor was on him.

A rush of energy, powered by fear, gave Tomas enough strength to respond. His body, trained by a lifetime of combat, acted as though it didn't even need his mind.

The obsidian knife cut left, right, up, and down, carving patterns in the air. The inquisitor's movements were quick, precise, and certain. Tomas retreated one step, then another, looking for an opening he wasn't sure would ever appear.

An idea exploded in his thoughts like the barrels outside the jail. This room had been the trap, and there was nothing stopping him from leaving. He'd left the door behind him wide open.

Tomas knew talented warriors who refused to retreat. Who met every challenge boldly and never backed down.

Most of them were buried next to the conscripts who'd never learned to properly wield a sword.

Tomas turned and ran.

Behind him, the inquisitor grunted and gave chase.

It was never a contest.

Tomas' legs were weak, his muscles burning. The inquisitor tackled him high across the waist, sending them both to the ground.

Tomas hit hard, knocking the breath from his lungs. He scrabbled and kicked with his feet, still fighting to reach the door. He reached with his hands, seeking any purchase that he could use to pull himself along. An inch at a time, the door grew bigger.

Tomas roared when the knife plunged through his back.

The inquisitor had missed his heart, but not by much. They both realized it. The inquisitor wiggled and twisted the knife, searching for the heart. Tomas tried to flip over. But between the inquisitor's blade and weight, he couldn't, no matter how he struggled.

Then something snapped.

Tomas spun, and he twisted until he was on his back.

Without warning, the pain in his back exploded, as though he'd been stabbed again. A scream ripped from Tomas' throat.

The inquisitor raised the obsidian knife to strike, but it was little more than a handle now with a jagged shard at the end.

Still, it was enough to beat a man to death with. The inquisitor struck, but Tomas deflected the arm away. Fire erupted across Tomas' back as he shifted. He swore he heard the broken blade scrape across the metal underneath him.

The inquisitor pushed down with his left arm, leaning more weight onto Tomas' chest. It drove the fragment of obsidian even deeper into Tomas' back, and Tomas could do nothing but scream as though the sound alone would save his life. He flailed at the man with his open hand, but the inquisitor casually shrugged off the haphazard blows.

The inquisitor pressed harder against Tomas' chest. When the fire again rippled across Tomas' back, the inquisitor punched down with his right hand again. Blinded by the agony, Tomas took the punch across the cheek. His head snapped right, but against the backdrop of pain, he barely noticed.

Once again, the training from his sword school took over. His masters expected him not only to be proficient with a sword, but empty-handed as well. He'd learned striking and grappling alongside cutting and parrying. He'd never been as useful without a sword, but the training held.

Tomas brought his arms in tight, protecting his head as best he could.

It helped. The inquisitor swung at him with both fists, but Tomas suffered no more than a few glancing blows.

The buzzing in his head grew louder, the bees multiplying as he fought. They were so loud Tomas couldn't even create a rational thought. Every move was instinct and old training instilled in his body.

The inquisitor switched tactics. He stopped punching and started driving his elbows down, breaking Tomas' guard. One elbow broke through cleanly, smashing into Tomas' forehead and slamming his head against the metal tunnel.

Blackness swarmed the edges of Tomas' vision. He raised his arms again, but the inquisitor formed a fist and punched Tomas right in the nose. Tomas heard the nose break, and warm blood spurted into his mouth as he gasped for air. He choked, coughed, and tried to spit, and the darkness closed in. The inquisitor laughed. "Owed you that," he said.

Tomas tried to raise his arms, but they wouldn't respond. Even his fingers refused his commands.

The inquisitor grinned and raised his hand for the killing blow. Tomas watched the man's hand twist. The final attack wouldn't be a punch, but a strike with the pommel of the knife.

A voice called out to him, familiar and yet distant.

Tomas closed his eyes, not interested in watching the final moments of his life.

The voice called again, louder, tinged with desperation.

He recognized it, even though the buzzing in his head was more violent than ever.

"Elzeth!" he called.

For just a moment, the sagani was there, a presence in his mind. He stood tall, a mirror image of Tomas, glowing brightly. He reached for Tomas, but Tomas couldn't bring himself to reach back. Even here, he was too tired.

He didn't want to die, but at least it would be quiet.

Elzeth shouted, a wordless scream. He lunged, and for a single moment, his hand brushed Tomas'.

Tomas' eyes snapped open. The inquisitor brought the pommel of his knife down, but it was slow.

Tomas didn't have long. The surge of strength had already begun to fade, the buzzing reverberating inside his skull. He struck at the only target he had, with all the strength remaining to him. His strike was faster, his stiff fingers reaching the inquisitor's throat before the pommel struck.

The inquisitor's eyes went wide, as did his strike. He dropped the knife handle and clutched at his throat with both hands.

Tomas searched the area around his head with his left hand. Numb fingers found the inquisitor's knife. It took Tomas two tries to wrap his hand around the grip. He raised it to his face and saw there wasn't much obsidian left. A sliver, perhaps as long as his finger was wide, remained. But it was sharp.

The inquisitor was still searching for air. Tomas wasn't sure his blow had been fatal, but he would take no chances. He groaned as he brought his knees up, planting his feet firmly on the ground.

Then he shouted, bridged, and twisted his hips.

The motion shoved the broken knife deeper into his shoulder, but the agony kept the darkness at bay, at least for a moment.

The inquisitor fell to the side, and Tomas rolled on top.

He was terribly positioned, but he hoped it didn't matter.

He switched the knife to his right hand and jammed the thumb and forefinger of his left hand into the inquisitor's eyes.

If the torturer screamed, Tomas couldn't hear it. The buzzing in his head left him deaf. The inquisitor grabbed at Tomas' left wrist with both hands, exposing himself.

Tomas stabbed what was left of the knife in the side of the inquisitor's neck.

It didn't cut far, but far enough. Blood pulsed out as Tomas withdrew the weapon.

He collapsed on top of the inquisitor, his head on the

man's chest. The churchman shuddered and spasmed, and then was still.

Tomas just lay there, not sure he would ever move again. He wasn't sure he wanted to. Hells, he was tired.

He didn't know how long he lay there. Perhaps a minute. It felt like an hour.

Clara made him move. He'd promised her a tea party.

She was still further inside.

He wasn't done yet.

40

Tomas pushed off his right arm, fighting his way to standing. The tunnel hummed and his head was worse than ever. His world tilted wildly as his knees threatened to buckle.

He half-stumbled, half-fell forward, his eyes on the switch at the end of the tunnel.

One step.

Then the next.

The switch was almost close enough to touch, but he didn't dare reach out, terrified that if he fell, he might never stand again.

He took a deep breath, even that sending a new wave of pain down his back. He took one big step and reached.

His leg quivered and finally surrendered. He pitched forward, desperately reaching for the switch.

His hand grasped the handle, and gravity did the rest of the work. He fell, pulling the switch down with him.

The buzzing in his head vanished. His sword clattered to the ground, coming to a rest near the inquisitor's body.

The humming in the background stopped, and Elzeth was there, the same as he had been day after day for almost as long as Tomas could remember.

Elzeth was swearing, a tirade that would have turned ears red in even the harshest taverns in the west.

Tears trickled down Tomas' face. He couldn't form words, not even as thoughts.

But it felt like an embrace from a long-lost friend.

Tomas no longer felt quite as weak as he had before, but he was still in no condition to fight. He couldn't reach the embedded obsidian, and there was a risk that if he moved too much, it would cut through something immediately fatal.

Also, so long as it was embedded, Elzeth couldn't heal the wounds.

But Clara and the others needed him. "I need you," he told Elzeth.

The sagani hesitated. "I'm not sure your body can take it."

Tomas coughed, spraying blood everywhere. "Doesn't much matter, does it?"

They rested together for a moment. After all their years, there was no need for debate.

They were together.

In this and in all things.

But Elzeth didn't burn. Something held him back, a flavor of hesitation Tomas didn't recognize.

"If we don't make it..." Elzeth said.

"Elzeth—"

"I just wanted to say, 'Thank you.'"

A lump formed in Tomas' throat. "You, too."

Elzeth burned then, bright enough to banish any fear.

Tomas stood. The pain was still there, but it was just pain. He flexed his hands, pleased to see they responded as he wished.

He walked back to his sword and picked it up, the familiar weight reassuring him as he held it.

"Best not to delay," Elzeth said. "Not sure how long your body will hold up."

Tomas nodded. He turned to the door the inquisitor had come from and threw it open.

The room beyond wasn't empty. There were devices, tall metal cylinders with glass windows. People stood inside the cylinders, their eyes lifeless.

One cylinder was open, a young boy within. Three adults fussed around him, doing something Tomas couldn't see.

Tomas walked toward them, crossing the small room in three quick steps.

He asked no questions, nor gave any quarter.

His sword cut through the crowd, dropping each of the adults without problem.

Whatever had happened here, though, he was already too late. The boy's chest didn't move, and his eyes were blank. Tomas didn't recognize him, but that hardly mattered.

He walked to each of the other cylinders and looked in.

Two of the cylinders held children, somewhere between twelve and fifteen, if Tomas had to guess. Their bodies were perfectly still.

The last cylinder held a full-grown woman, but like the others, she was dead.

Another table, like the one in the room behind him, stood in the center of this room. Its presence mocked him, as though knowing it held secrets it would never reveal. Other tables were smaller, holding more surgical instruments.

Still no Clara, though. Or any of the other missing children.

The space couldn't be much larger. It was already an impressive feat of construction, and there hadn't been that many bunks in the room behind him.

There was another door, and Tomas went to it, wondering what fresh nightmare waited on the other side.

Tomas opened the door, and once again was surprised. Here there were no operating tables. He saw no metal cylinders, no surgical implements. The room was smaller than any of the others, and yet had more character than the rest of the hideout combined. An expensive desk dominated the room, and books lined shelves everywhere.

In the corner of the room, several of the children huddled in the corner, whimpering softly. The children from Ben's place. All that were still unaccounted for.

Standing just behind the desk was a tall, thin man that Tomas had never seen. From the quality of his clothes and the immaculate condition of his nails, he immediately struck Tomas as a man who'd never seen a day of honest labor in his life.

He held Clara tightly, his left arm wrapped around her. His right hand held a knife, already digging into her throat.

"This one said you would come. Insisted on it, actually," the man said. Tomas had heard the voice before. The one who ran this place, the one who had come into Callum's inn and offered the bounty for Tomas' head.

The man shifted his weight, and Tomas heard a soft click of a switch flipping. Something he'd done with his foot.

"I didn't believe her. I thought Zachary would be enough, especially in that tunnel. Tell me, how did you defeat him?"

The man seemed genuinely curious, as though it were the most natural question in the world.

When Tomas didn't answer, the man frowned. "Very well, then. Regardless, it must have been some fight. You're not looking very good, Tomas."

Tomas gripped his sword tighter. The knife was too close to Clara's neck, and the desk was no small obstacle.

The man continued, not bothered by the fact he was the only one talking. "No doubt you heard what I did. I believe you demons have very sharp hearing. This whole place has been rigged with explosives, on the slim chance we were ever discovered. I've just lit a fuse that can't be stopped. In five minutes, this place will no longer exist."

The children cried louder, and the man shot them a disdainful look. "If you wish to save these children, you will let me and little Clara here go. Once I am safely up top, I will drop the key to the cells down to you. If you act quickly, you should be able to get everyone free."

"And if not?"

"You will not find the key in time," the man said. "And you will doom these children to being buried alive."

"But you'll be dead, too."

The man shrugged. "I am willing to die to defeat the scourge of demons that you represent. Are you willing to die here, with all these children for company?"

It was the lack of bluster that convinced Tomas. The man wasn't desperate or trying to prove a point, even to himself. He was willing to die here, if necessary.

And no enemy was more dangerous than one willing to sacrifice everything to win.

The man pressed the knife harder into Clara's throat, drawing blood.

"The clock is ticking, Tomas. What will you choose?"

41

S weat formed on Tomas' forehead and trickled down. Each heartbeat thudded in his chest, counting down time he didn't have.

Across the desk, the man seemed to be in no hurry. His eyes were clear, his stance steady. Tomas knew his opponent was no warrior. But he held every advantage, and he was ready to die.

Tomas hated believers.

The children's cries grew, and the man shushed them. His gaze never left Tomas.

"What will it be?" he asked.

Tomas looked to the children in the corner, then back to the man, and then down at Clara.

Despite her predicament, she didn't cry.

Her look was the worst of them all.

She looked at him with hope in her eyes. She believed he could save them all.

Tomas didn't believe the man intended to let them live through the night. Once he was free, he would betray his word.

Which only left one choice.

The discussion between him and Elzeth was a wordless one, their emotions communicating all they needed.

Tomas' request was logical enough. Elzeth's hesitation reasonable.

But no options remained.

Tomas tore down the barriers that remained between him and Elzeth. Thought disappeared, replaced by a pure, burning anger.

Tomas had underestimated the rage Elzeth carried. The sagani was disgusted at the treatment of the children, at the crimes that had been committed at the behest of this man. With the barriers down, Elzeth's righteous rage became Tomas' own, lending him a sharpness of focus he'd never before experienced in unity.

When Tomas stepped forward, it was as if the scene was frozen in time.

Two paces brought him halfway across the room, and the man's eyes were just beginning to widen. Tomas felt every muscle in his back as the embedded obsidian blade sliced deeper into it.

Now, though, it was just one way of many to die.

Tomas had gambled, and in the next moment, it paid off.

The man was no warrior. Though he didn't flinch from giving the order to kill, he probably hadn't done much himself. Killing Clara would have been a conscious act, a decision made in some fraction of a second.

But defending himself was instinctive, a reaction deep in his body.

The man started to bring the knife away from Clara's neck, trying to defend against Tomas.

Tomas leaped over the desk and cut as he passed. His blade passed an inch over Clara's head. The man should have chosen a taller hostage. Tomas' sword sliced clean through the man's neck, separating the vertebrae as though they'd been connected by no more than a piece of string.

Tomas landed before the man's head began to topple.

Elzeth built the barriers between them once again, afraid that in their current condition, unity might be permanent.

Clara broke free of the man's dead grip and ran for Tomas, wrapping him in an embrace.

"We need to get out of here," Tomas croaked.

Clara nodded, then startled as the man's body finally toppled. Tomas shuffled over to him and searched his pockets. He found the key easily.

Where else would such a man hide something? He would only trust it on his person.

Tomas looked back down to Clara. "Clara, I need you to be brave. I need you to lead all these children out of here. Just keep going straight. Eventually, there's a ladder you'll need to climb. Can you get them all out?"

She nodded, her eyes wide. "You'll save the others?"

"I will."

She set her jaw and marched over to the other children. In a voice much louder than necessary, she said, "Line up! Hands at your sides, no pushing!"

If he didn't hurt so much, Tomas would have laughed. She sounded just like Ben.

An inquisitor turned caretaker.

The children stopped their whimpering and stood up, arranging themselves in a rough line. Clara turned and marched, and after a moment of hesitation, the others followed.

Tomas brought up the rear. Every step caused the pain in his back to build, but he could ignore it long enough to get this key in the cell door. The children marched through the room with the cylinders and into the tunnel. They picked up speed the longer they walked. Tomas fought the urge to shudder as he passed through the tunnel, but the body of the inquisitor brought him great comfort. He spit blood on the body as he passed.

Soon, he was in front of the cells, the children within staring as the smaller children marched past.

Tomas put the key in the lock and turned it, breathing a sigh of relief when it turned without difficulty.

He ushered the rest of the children out. With the older ones helping, the evacuation moved even faster. One by one, the children climbed the ladder and disappeared from Tomas' sight.

Tomas returned to the room with the tables, where the boy was still unconscious. He swore, knowing how much this would hurt. He picked the child up and slung him over his shoulder. The fresh pain almost brought him to his knees, but he refused to fall.

Not here, not after all this. One step at a time, he made his way to the ladder.

It couldn't be more than a dozen feet up, but it looked like the tallest mountain he'd ever seen.

Above him, the children all poked their heads over the lip. When they saw him, they cheered him on.

Tomas grabbed the first rung with his right hand. He stepped up, made sure he was balanced, then released the ladder and grabbed it quickly again, one rung higher.

Every rung brought a new wave of agony. His body felt like it would simply shatter into pieces with every move.

But the children's cheers pulled him higher. He wanted to shout at them to run, but hadn't the breath.

Then he was at the top. The children were all there

when he emerged, several of them pulling on him and the boy to help get them both all the way out. He wasn't sure he could have done it without them.

It wasn't over, though, not quite yet.

The man's threat echoed in his memory.

"Run to the farmhouse!" he shouted and led the way at a shuffling gait. He pulled the boy behind him, several of the other children helping.

They were only halfway to the farmhouse when the ground behind them erupted. The ground shook, throwing Tomas and several of the youngest children down. The soil collapsed as the explosions came closer and closer to Tomas.

He had no energy left to move. He watched the ground fall away, the long hole coming closer and closer to swallowing him up.

It stopped ten paces away from him.

The explosions stopped and the world went quiet once again. Tomas blinked, unable to believe how close they'd come to being trapped forever. If they'd been a minute slower—

He didn't even want to think about it.

He leaned back, looked up at the dark sky, and swore.

Clara, still beside him, looked over and waggled her finger, her expression serious. "Ben says you're not allowed to use that word."

And even though it hurt so much, Tomas laughed.

42

Tomas woke to the sounds of a young town already busy for the day, fighting to establish itself in a hostile land. The bed next to him was empty, the marshal of the town as occupied as the merchants. He knew he should move, and yet the warmth of the sun shining through the windows made him want to stay here forever.

He thought about Angela, and specifically about last night. Today would make five days he had been cooped up in her house. The first three he didn't remember much of. After a doctor pulled the obsidian blade from his back and bandaged him up, Angela had brought him here, where he'd fallen promptly asleep.

He'd woken a few times, but for the most part he rested and healed. Elzeth was quiet and content, glowing with the satisfaction of the work they'd done.

They had both needed the rest.

Yesterday had been the first day he'd been awake and active. Elzeth had repaired his body, and Tomas had thought to explore the town and maybe visit Ben.

Angela asked him not to. Tension lingered throughout

Razin. The mission had lost its priest, and the believers in town were distraught. Several of the merchants, skittish after a night of explosions in town, were ready to leave at the slightest hint of trouble, and she worried he would be the spark that sent her town over the edge. Her only remaining deputy was an injured Veric, and she knew she couldn't handle even the smallest problems now.

He'd agreed, partly as a favor to her, but partly because he wanted to test his healing before risking anyone's ire. So, while she was at work, he'd stretched and exercised, running through the forms of his school until the sweat poured from his body.

As near as he could tell, he possessed no lingering damage. He watched himself for tics all day and studied his own thoughts, but nothing alarmed him.

Once again, he had pushed himself to the brink and returned unharmed. It made no sense, and yet there was nothing to do but accept it.

When Angela reappeared, late last night, something had changed. She tried to hide it from him, but she wasn't that good at concealing her emotions. From the way she kept glancing at him when she thought he wasn't looking, he knew it was about him, too.

She had been fierce that night, as though trying to say something with her body she wasn't sure how to say out loud.

It had been another of the best nights of his life. But he feared what it meant.

Lacking anything better to do, he ran through his forms again.

He hadn't gotten very far when there was a knock on Angela's door. Elzeth sharpened Tomas' hearing, and Tomas heard a familiar voice softly say, "It's me, Tomas. Angela asked me to come."

Tomas walked to the front door and opened it, letting Ben in. He closed the door quickly, and after Ben took off his boots, led him to the table in the dining room. The older man walked slowly, his injuries still troubling him. He looked at Tomas with wonder. "Sometimes, I think it's not fair, what you can do. You had both feet in the grave when I saw you last."

Tomas shrugged. "You know how to attain it."

Ben shook his head. "The cost isn't worth it." He grunted as he sat down. "And truthfully, what you have frightens me. I may not be an inquisitor anymore, but I'm still not certain that a host is natural or right. I'm content to be human, and to hopefully die a frail old man."

Tomas nodded, but wasn't in the mood for such a conversation. "You're not here to lend me your wisdom."

"I'm not," Ben agreed. "Angela wanted me to tell you what we've found."

Tomas leaned forward. Last night, Angela had said Ben was helping with the excavation, but she hadn't said more. He didn't understand why she would send Ben.

"To answer the obvious question first," Ben said, "we've found little to nothing that would tell us what experiments they were running. We've dug up most of the rooms, and anything useful was blasted. We've found surgical instruments, the cells, and food, but nothing that leads us to an answer. They were running experiments, but of what kind, we couldn't say. They needed human subjects. And, given that it was the church, I'm sure the sagani are tied in somehow. But I'm not telling you anything you hadn't already guessed." He looked up at the ceiling. "I'm most curious about those tubes, but they're nothing but twisted metal now."

"There was a long tunnel that disrupted my connection with Elzeth."

Ben's eyes narrowed at that fact. "We found the tunnel, as well as wires running around it. But it was one of the places where an enormous amount of explosive was planted."

"So, we know nothing."

Ben held up a placating hand. "You saved those children. If you accomplished nothing else, it was still far more than enough."

He ran a hand through his thinning hair. "The body is a wreck, but we found the person you killed. The person Clara says was in charge. I saw him, when he attacked my home." Ben paused. "It made me freeze when they came."

"You know him?"

"His name is Rychard. He was a cardinal."

"Oh." Tomas couldn't come up with anything else to say in response. He leaned back in his chair. The pieces all fell into place, and he understood why Ben was here. His stomach twisted. "You told Angela yesterday, didn't you?"

Ben nodded.

Tomas looked out the window, his thoughts a jumbled mess. "Is there anything else?"

Ben shook his head.

"Thank you for telling me."

"He was a terrible man."

Tomas inclined his head, but his heart hurt again, almost as if he'd been stabbed.

Silence stretched between them.

After a few minutes, Ben stood up. He bowed deeply to Tomas. "I do not know if our paths will ever cross again.

And so, I'll say this one more time. Thank you. From the bottom of my heart, I will always thank you for what you've done for me and for the children. If there is ever anything I can do, all you have to do is ask."

"Live in peace, Ben. There's nothing more I could hope for."

Ben's eyes glistened, but he nodded one last time, then made his way out.

Tomas sat in the chair, looking out the window, his heart a heavy rock in his chest.

43

Tomas sat in that chair for the rest of the morning. The sun rose, shifting the shadows in the room. The air smelled like Angela, like she was still here standing next to him.

"Want to talk?" Elzeth asked.

"Not really," Tomas said.

He felt Elzeth's acknowledgment. "I'm sorry."

"Me too. But nothing for it, right?"

Elzeth grunted, and the pair lapsed again into silence.

Angela came home earlier than the night before. She brought fresh food from one of the caravans. She took one look at him and knew. "Ben stopped by?"

"He did."

She stood in her own house, as though uncertain if she belonged. Tomas got up. "Is the food for us?"

She nodded.

"Then let's not let it go to waste."

She just stood there, frozen. "Tomas—"

He held up his hand to stop her. "I know. Not yet."

It took her a moment, but then she understood. She

forced a smile onto her face. She brought the food into the kitchen, and together they cooked supper.

As they did, she talked about her day. The churchgoers were frightened, the merchants were skittish, and some young boy was harassing women in the street. The town remained on edge, but one step at a time, was backing away from disaster. Angela balanced it all, telling how she'd placated those who were nervous and reassured those who were ready to leave.

Veric was back on his feet, and together they were just managing to hold the town together.

Through it all, they cooked. Tomas asked questions and poked fun at some of the problems she had to solve. Gradually, Angela's shoulders relaxed, and the smile on her face was no longer forced.

Tomas felt much the same. If he focused hard on just this moment, he could almost convince himself this was normal. That he and Angela were just another man and woman, coming together after a long day of working apart.

For the first time, it wasn't hard for him to imagine that future. It tasted sweet, and weighed his heart down even more.

They drank wine with the meal and talked until the sun went down.

With the meal finished, she looked at him, and the smile fell from her face. "They'll hunt you down as soon as they know."

"I know."

She looked down at her empty wine glass, as though wishing it were full again. Then she took a deep breath and said, "I could go with you."

He smiled. "Thank you." He twirled his own glass by the

stem. "But your duty is here. You've built something good, and it still needs tending. I understand."

The tension dropped from her body again. "I would have, if you'd asked."

"That means the world to me." He gestured around the room. "For what it's worth, I never thought I could consider settling someplace with people. Not until I came here."

She bowed her head, letting her hair cover her face. After a moment, she wiped her eyes, then looked up and met his gaze. "Where will you go?"

"Don't know," he said. "And even if I did, I think it would be better for you if I didn't say. You'll need to be careful, too."

She looked like a child upset they were being given an obvious rule.

Then she stood up and put her glass down. "Come on," she said, and walked to the bedroom.

Later, when she was asleep, Tomas sat up and perched on the edge of the bed. He looked back and saw her, sheets tangled in a mess, and he swore he saw a hint of a smile on her face. "Never let me forget this," he said.

Elzeth agreed, and Tomas stood and got dressed.

After he put on his boots he stopped, his hand quivering as he reached to open the door.

What kind of person was he, to leave this all behind?

Years ago, he would have killed for this opportunity.

Remaining risked her life and his. More than that, it risked the peace of the town she'd worked so hard to build and protect.

If anyone could protect them, though, it was him. Time and time again, he'd risen to the challenges life had put in his way.

He looked back through the house, just able to make out her legs in the bed.

He turned back.

Only a fool would leave.

"Tomas," Elzeth said.

He stopped, frozen between two futures.

"We need to go. You've seen what the church is capable of, and you can't protect her, too."

Elzeth was right. Tomas knew it, but turning his back on Angela was the hardest thing he could remember doing. Harder by far than his fight against the inquisitor.

He turned the handle and left Angela's house. He kept her key, though.

No one saw him as he left town. The alleys were quiet, people tucked into their houses. Tomas escaped the outskirts, and before long he was in the prairie once again. He walked until he could barely see Razin, then turned to give it one last look.

"You did the right thing," Elzeth said.

"Feels like hell."

"It does." The sagani laughed. "At least you've still got me."

Tomas scoffed. "You're not nearly as pretty."

"I'm sure that among my kind I was considered quite beautiful."

Tomas didn't even know what to say to that, so he didn't encourage that line of conversation. "Well, if I'm stuck with you, why don't you decide which direction we go next?"

Elzeth thought for a moment. "How about north?"

"North?" Tomas frowned. "You sure? Winter's not that far off."

"Maybe the cold will scare the church away."

Tomas laughed out loud at that. "After we killed a cardinal? They'd pursue us into the fires of all three hells."

Elzeth turned serious, and Tomas felt an echo of the

rage he'd felt in the bunkers. They'd killed the cardinal, but Elzeth's need for justice wasn't sated yet. "Let them come," he said.

Tomas looked up at the stars and found the way north. He started walking.

"Let them come," he agreed.

THE ADVENTURES CONTINUE!

Top o' the morning!

I hope that wherever you are in the world, and whenever it is you're reading this, that you're doing well.

First, as an author, let me thank you for reading *A Sword Named Vengeance*. Whether this is the first book of mine you've read or my twentieth, I hope that you enjoyed it. There have never been more ways to be entertained, and it truly means the world to me that you choose to spend your time in these pages.

If you enjoyed the story, rest assured the Tomas' and Elzeth's next adventure isn't far off. Keep an eye out for the next book, releasing soon!

And if you're looking to spread the word, there's few better ways to support the story by leaving a review where you purchased the book!

Thanks again!

Ryan

STAY IN TOUCH

Thanks once again for reading *Eyes of the Hidden World*. I had a tremendous amount of fun writing this story, and am looking forward to writing more of Tomas and Elzeth.

If you enjoyed the story, I'd ask that you consider signing up to get emails from me. You can do so at:

www.waterstonemedia.net/newsletter

I typically email readers once or twice a month, and one of my greatest pleasures over the past five years has been getting to know the people reading my stories.

If I'm being honest, email is my favorite way of communicating with readers. Whether it's hearing from soldiers stationed overseas or grandmothers tending to their gardens, email has allowed me to make new friends all over the world.

Email subscribers also get all the goodies. From free books in all formats, to sample chapters and surprise short stories, if I'm giving something away, it's through email.

I hope you'll join us.

Ryan

ALSO BY RYAN KIRK

Saga of the Broken Gods

Band of Broken Gods

Last Sword in the West

Last Sword in the West

Eyes of the Hidden World

Oblivion's Gate

The Gate Beyond Oblivion

The Gates of Memory

The Gate to Redemption

Relentless

Relentless Souls

Heart of Defiance

Their Spirit Unbroken

The Nightblade Series

Nightblade

World's Edge

The Wind and the Void

Blades of the Fallen

Nightblade's Vengeance

Nightblade's Honor

Nightblade's End

Standalone Novels

Blades of Shadow

The Primal Series

Primal Dawn

Primal Darkness

Primal Destiny

ABOUT THE AUTHOR

Ryan Kirk is the bestselling author of the *Nightblade* series of books. When he isn't writing, you can probably find him playing disc golf or hiking through the woods.

www.waterstonemedia.net
contact@waterstonemedia.net

 facebook.com/waterstonemedia
twitter.com/waterstonebooks
instagram.com/waterstonebooks